S0-BBM-468

THE SECRET ON RUM RUNNER'S LANE

THE SECRET ON RUM RUNNER'S LANE

A BOOK MAGIC MINI MYSTERY

MELISSA BOURBON

Copyright © 2020 by Melissa Bourbon

All rights reserved.

No part of this book may be reproduced in any form or by any electronic
or mechanical means, including information storage and retrieval systems,
without written permission from the author, except for the use of brief
quotations in a book review.

This is a work of fiction. Names, characters, places, and incidents either
are the product of the author's imagination or are used fictitiously, and any
resemblance to actual persons, living or dead, business establishments,
events, or locales is entirely coincidental.

Print Book ISBN 978-0-9978661-5-5

Ebook ASIN B088J48JY8

Published by Lake House Press

Art by Dar Albert, Wicked Smart Designs

Join my newsletter mailing list and receive a free exclusive copy of *The Bookish Kitchen*, a compilation of recipes from my different series.

This one's for you, Mary Crooks.

PRAISE FOR THE BOOK MAGIC MYSTERIES

"A combination of magic and mystery, "Murder In Devil's Cove" by Melissa Bourbon is a deftly crafted and impressively original novel by an author with a genuine flair for originality. While certain to be an unusual, immediate and enduringly popular addition to community library Mystery/Suspense collections, it should be noted for the personal reading lists of anyone who enjoys Women's Friendship Fiction, Cozy Animal Mysteries, or Supernatural Mysteries..."

—Midwest Book Review

"The unraveling of the mystery involves Pippin's family history (it goes all the way back to Roman times in Ireland), hidden clues, a long-lost keepsake, and a secret room. For mystery fans who enjoy amateur detectives who rely on mystical insights rather than Holmesian deductions, Murder in Devil's Cove will provide an entertaining read."

—Seattle Book Review

"A magical blend of books, mystery, and smart sleuthing. Melissa Bourbon's Murder in Devil's Cove offers mystery readers everything they crave and stands out in the crowded cozy genre. This captivating new series will leave readers spellbound."

~NYT and USA Today Bestselling Author, Ellery Adams

"This tightly woven mystery spins a web of intrigue where magic simmers, waiting for the perfect time to surface. I can't wait to read more about Pippin and what awaits her in the next Book Magic adventure."

~Dru Ann Love, Dru's Book Musings

Praise for Murder in Devil's Cove

This book had me at 'book magic' and wrapped me up in its unique plot from start to finish! . . . I really enjoyed the set-up, the plot, the characters and the setting; they all added intriguing layers to the story. . .

~Reading Is My SuperPower

I thought the author beautifully intertwined magic and mystery...Murder in Devil's Cove is an intriguing tale with forbidden books, a departed dad, family folklore, mysterious magic, renovation revelations, and one bewildered bibliomancer.

~The Avid Reader

This book totally sucked me in as the story tells the past as well as the present . . . a truly magical read for fans of cozies with a slight magical flair.

I totally loved it so I give it 5/5 stars.

~Books a Plenty Book Reviews

Filled with quirky characters and atmospheric descriptions of the quaint town of Devil's Cove, Bourbon hits all the right notes for a cozy: amateur sleuthing, several possible suspects, bookstores, and a touch of romance.

~Elena Taylor, Author

Blending a family curse and a hint of the paranormal with an intriguing mystery MURDER IN DEVIL'S COVE is a fantastic start to a new series.

~*Cozy Up With Kathy*

Praise for The Secret on Rum Runner's Lane

The Secret on Rum Runner's Lane by Melissa Bourbon is a fantastical book that I loved diving into. It was great from the first chapter to the ending.

~*Baroness' Book Trove*

This is the prequel to this new series and it had me hooked on the concept, the setting. and the characters.

~*Storeybook Reviews*

It may be a short story but it gives a thorough introduction of the characters as well as a picturesque view of Devil's Cove. Sure to pique the interest of cozy lovers looking for a mini-mystery to draw them into a new series.

~*Books a Plenty Book Reviews*

. . . this was a quick read about characters that you immediately care about in a picturesque setting (two, actually).

~*I Read What You Write!*

THE SECRET ON RUM RUNNER'S LANE captures the uncertainty and underlying strength of women searching for their place in the world. It allows readers to get a glimpse of the past while seeing the glimmer of what's to come.

~*Cozy Up With Kathy*

The Secret on Rum Runner's Lane is a layered story with a well-developed backstory for a character whose decisions in that time period set the path for generations to come.

~*Reading Is My SuperPower*

The setting is enchanting with realistic characters you can root for. The mystery is perfectly solvable based on the clues hidden within the text. The paranormal aspect is an original idea.

~*Diane Reviews Books*

The author brings the story to life with her character development and vivid setting. I could feel Cassie's pain dealing with her family curse. I was totally transported into her world.

~*Socrates' Book Reviews...*

The Lane Family

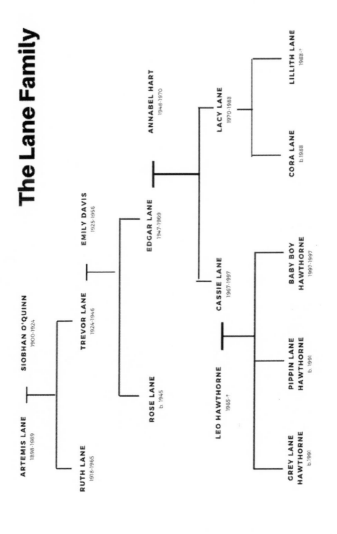

ARTEMIS LANE
1898-1969

SIOBHAN O'QUINN
1900-1924

RUTH LANE
1918-1965

TREVOR LANE
1924-1946

EMILY DAVIS
1925-1956

ROSE LANE
b. 1945

EDGAR LANE
1947-1969

ANNABEL HART
1948-1970

CASSIE LANE
1967-1997

LACY LANE
1970-1988

CORA LANE
b. 1988

LILLITH LANE
1988-?

LEO HAWTHORNE
1965-?

GREY LANE
HAWTHORNE
b.1991

PIPPIN LANE
HAWTHORNE
b. 1991

BABY BOY
HAWTHORNE
1997-1997

THE SECRET ON RUM RUNNER'S LANE

"Books. They are lined up on shelves or stacked on a table. There they are wrapped up in their jackets, lines of neat print on nicely bound pages. They look like such orderly, static things. Then you, the reader come along. You open the book jacket, and it can be like opening the gates to an unknown city, or opening the lid of a treasure chest. You read the first word and you're off on a journey of exploration and discovery."

~David Almond

Chapter 1

"When I visit the cemetery, I walk past hundreds, possibly thousands of stories now silenced. And I know that history 'recorded' holds the adventures that history 'lost' let slip through its fingers. And I've thought that I need to live a life worthy of being 'recorded' so that the adventure that might help another never slips through the fingers of anything."

~ Craig D. Lounsbrough

*L*aurel Point. It was a spit of a town nestled between a forest of evergreens and the vast Pacific Ocean, a place stuck in time. Quaint, most people said, but to Cassandra Lane it had become stifling.

Laurel Point wasn't precisely home for Cassie. She'd grown up on the outskirts—on Cape Misery.

Being stuck on the cape was isolating. On top of that, she was burdened with a fate from which she wanted—no, needed—to escape.

She couldn't wait to get away from the everything Cape Misery represented.

She couldn't wait to get away from the *magic*.

From the moment they could verbalize, and possibly even before, Cassandra and Lacy Lane had known they were different from other people. For starters, they had no mother and no father. Oh, of course, they'd *come* from a union between two people, but Edgar had died in a tragic fishing accident in 1969. Later that same year, when Cassie was just three years old, Annabel died giving birth to Lacy.

The weight of responsibility for their mother's death lay heavy on Lacy, though Cassie never blamed her. The fact was, Annabel and Edgar had fallen victim to the Lane family curse: the men were taken by the sea and the women lost their lives during childbirth.

It simply was the way things were. The sisters' fate was written. They had vowed from the beginning to never fall in love and to never, ever—under any circumstance, get pregnant.

The Lane sisters didn't live in an ordinary house in an ordinary town. Instead, they lived in the lighthouse on Cape Misery. Edgar and Annabel, in the decade before they'd died, had taken over the family's lighthouse, turning it into the bookstore it now was.

"How many kids can say they live in a lighthouse?" Cassie asked her sister at least once a year, trying to make it sound more exciting than it was. "Not many," Lacy always answered with a smile. She didn't seem to mind the isolation. She immersed herself in the volumes shelved in Books by Bequest, happy as a pirate with a jug of Jamaican rum.

Cassie didn't want her classmates to whisper about her behind her back, but they did it anyway. The girls came from a family of bibliomancers, and while the townspeople visited Aunt Rose for guidance in the way one might see a therapist, the town's kids made fun of what they didn't understand.

"Witch!" some hollered.

"Unnatural!" others said, mimicking what their parents said in the privacy of their own homes.

Cassie and Lacy had each other. That had to be enough.

When Edgar and Annabel both died, the girls' eccentric Aunt Rose took over their upbringing. Rose was the only mother the girls had ever known. She was their rock, even if her presence in their lives was more an ever-shifting tidal pool than a sturdy, unyielding lighthouse.

As she grew up, Cassie's favorite spot in the world was the bench at the top of the hill near her parents' graves. When she sat on the bench, the Lane family graveyard was to her left. To her right and down the hill was the white stone tower that was the lighthouse, with its arched wooden door, red reflectors, and black iron accents at the windows. The blue expanse of the Pacific Ocean lay beyond, its white-caps churning wildly, its secrets buried, never to be revealed.

The small cemetery was dotted with gravestones made from slate or sandstone. Each of the tablet stones was placed vertically at the head of its particular plot, a few tilted one way or the other, but most were upright, standing sentry to the souls of the people buried beneath. Cassie supposed it was because of this little graveyard that she'd come to love the earth so much. The flowers that bordered the picket fence around the space. The flowers she and Aunt Rose planted alongside each headstone every spring while Lacy holed up inside Books by Bequest, reading every ancient tome she could get her hands on.

This was the core difference between her and Lacy. Lacy loved the family's gift of bibliomancy. She loved books, the stories they told, the secrets they held, and the future they predicted, while Cassie preferred life outside and the way flowers in the spring gave the promise of a new tomorrow and how the falling leaves in autumn meant a cleansing of the soul and a time to reflect and rebuild. She *wished* she could read the books in the store, but the truth was, she didn't trust the messages the books gave, and she didn't want to glimpse the future. Lately she'd begun to wonder if Lacy trusted them, either. So many times, Cassie had seen Lacy absorbed in her divination, gleaning messages about the past, or predictions about the future, only to see frustration take hold as Lacy slammed closed the book that had been open in her lap, or on the table before her, or on the pillow of her bed.

Cassie had eventually become convinced that the Lane women's divination was actually another part of the curse that plagued her family. Teaching them how to use their gift of bibliomancy had been Aunt Rose's greatest joy when the sisters were younger, but now she furrowed her brows at Lacy when the books didn't tell her what she wanted to hear, and at Cassie when she refused to even pick up a book. "I don't want to know," Cassie would say, and Aunt Rose would nod as if she understood, but deep down, Cassie knew she didn't. Aunt Rose wondered how a person could deny such a big part of herself, and though she worried about Lacy getting lost in it, she also worried that Cassie having nothing to do with it would end badly.

Because, Aunt Rose always told the girls, you can't run from who and what you are.

But that was exactly what Cassie was going to do. The first opportunity she had, she was getting away from Cape Misery. Away from Oregon. Putting her past behind her.

Leaving Lacy, Aunt Rose, Annabel and Edgar, and the

lighthouse wouldn't be easy, but it was essential, because no book was going to tell Cassie what her future held. This place that tried to hem her in with its coastal fog, its isolating cape, its stone-walled lighthouse—this place would not contain her.

She was going to make her own destiny.

GROWING UP, Cassie had a natural propensity to act as the protector of her little sister, who never, ever wanted protecting.

When Cassie tried to brush Lacy's hair, Lacy would snatch the brush and run across the room, saying, "I can take care of myself, thank you very much."

When Cassie wanted to hold Lacy's hand as they found their footing on the jagged rocks along the shore, Lacy would pull free, scurrying along at a dizzying pace, with reckless abandon that made Cassie hold her breath and pray.

When Lacy proclaimed that she would defy the Lane curse and become a mother, Cassie made a pact with her, right then and there, a promise that neither one would ever get pregnant.

And when Cassie tried to get Lacy to come up to the graveyard with her to talk to their parents, Lacy eschewed the very idea. "I talk to them in the books," she claimed.

Despite their differences, they were thick as thieves, as Aunt Rose always said. Even though she wouldn't let Cassie touch her locks, Lacy always wanted to brush Cassie's hair, and she dragged Cassie with her to the beach to see a blinking light far out at the horizon, sure it was a morse code message from one of the Lane ancestors.

The sisters even looked alike—both petite and with eyes that were as blue as the cerulean skies above. Cassie's hair was blonder, with a touch of strawberry like their mother's, or so they were told, while Lacy's had the brown tint of their father's. Both had curls that bounced and framed their faces like wispy halos that became instant bird's nests of leaves and twigs when the wind came, which was often living on the Oregon coast. Their curls had still been the envy of every schoolgirl they'd ever encountered. The jealousy of schoolgirls was not to be taken lightly and had stuck with them throughout their adolescence. Another line on Cassie's list of reasons to leave.

They both steered clear of eating any living thing that came from the sea, fearful that their ancestors' blood coursed through the bottom-feeding shrimp or the white-fleshed halibut. They cooked the meals for their little family because Aunt Rose lost track of time, and if Cassie and Lacy had left meal preparations to her, they'd have eaten a breakfast of leathering steak at midnight and a dinner of runny scrambled eggs at four in the afternoon.

Cassie found the recipes, wrote them out by hand so as not to depend on an open book, and added the ingredients to Aunt Rose's market list. Then she and Lacy would prepare the meals together, each working through the steps, moving around each other wordlessly, as if they'd done it a thousand times. By the time they were in their teens, it felt as if they had.

Where Cassie cooked by using precise measurements, Lacy, let loose in the kitchen. She was like a chemist—or, Cassie thought wryly, like a witch. Lacy tossed handfuls of herbs or flours or whatever she was drawn to into a boiling pot of soup as if it were a cauldron and she was crafting the potion to end all potions.

They were opposites, but they complemented one another like dark chocolate and red wine, or salt and caramel.

They'd been parentless, but Aunt Rose had done her very best. She'd never had children of her own, and inheriting Cassie and Lacy had been unexpected. Truth be told, Aunt Rose had been ill-equipped to raise the sisters. She practiced her bibliomancy for the same people in the town whose children steered clear of her nieces, and for the people who came to Books by Bequest explicitly to get a "reading". She lived in her books more than she lived in the real world.

Cassie became the keeper of the schedule and her organization was the thing that kept her and Lacy on track, despite Lacy's wild tendencies. But now, with Lacy sixteen, nearly seventeen, and Cassie nineteen, nearly twenty, their paths were clear. Lacy could have her books. Cassie would take flowers and fresh air any day of the week.

Cassie stood now, brushing dirt from her knees and peeling off her garden gloves. She left the flat of impatiens, only half planted, and walked into the fenced area and right up to Annabel and Edgar's graves. A black crow perched on the one of the headstones. It always appeared when she felt uncertain about her decisions or her future. She saw it as a symbol of her personal transformation. Its presence now reinforced what she wanted to tell her parents. She spoke to them whenever she needed an ear, which lately was nearly every day.

If only Annabel and Edgar could answer.

"I'm still here," she usually said, followed by a hasty, "but I can't leave you...or Lacy...or Aunt Rose."

Sometimes the leaves on the trees would rustle and

Cassie would imagine that the breeze was Annabel trying to hug her.

Most often, there was just silence.

This time though, Cassie was actually saying goodbye. More than anything, Lacy didn't want Cassie's mothering anymore. Something had caused her sister to shut her out, and Aunt Rose had her books and her divination.

It was time.

Cassie had just opened her mouth to speak—to tell her parents that this time she was really going—when a scream came from somewhere below. Her heart shot into her throat. Was it from the lighthouse, or had it carried up from the beach? Was it Aunt Rose or...oh no, was it—?

"Lacy!" she yelled. She started to run, but her legs felt like they were moving in slow motion.

The scream came again, this time followed by a string of cursing. Cassie stopped in her tracks. Closed her eyes. "Oh, thank God," she whispered. It *was* Lacy, but she wasn't in trouble. Probably some book had given her a glimpse into a past or a future she didn't want to see. That was par for the course. Lately Lacy's abilities seemed to fail her more and more.

Now Cassie went back to her parents. "It's just Lacy," she said with a sigh. It felt like a refrain she kept repeating lately: "It's just Lacy."

LATER THAT NIGHT, as Cassie lay in bed, she tried to pinpoint the moment things had started to spiral out of control.

First, a book set in Czechoslovakia about a womanizing man, his sad wife, and his mistress mysteriously appeared. It had been leaned up against the front door of the lighthouse.

There had been no note, and there had been no clue about who'd left it.

And second, according to Lacy, that book foretold a betrayal.

Cassie's betrayal of Lacy.

"What does that even mean?" Cassie demanded. Lacy gave no context. No information. No specific details.

"You're going to hurt me more than anyone else ever has or will," Lacy said, as if that explained everything.

"I would never betray you!" Cassie had just stared at her sister, wide-eyed and, frankly, flabbergasted. They'd always had each other, so the chasm that divided them now, that had carved itself into the granite that had been their sisterhood, felt like a chisel chipping away at Cassie's heart.

She swiped away the tears pooling in her eyes and rolled over. The book left by a stranger that day had caused an impenetrable cocoon to instantly form. The appeasing words Cassie repeatedly tossed out to her sister inevitably bounced back in an unending volley Cassie would never win.

If there was one word to describe Lacy, it was pigheaded. If she could pick a few more, she'd say her sister was willful, obstinate, and downright mulish.

"I am not going to betray you," Cassie repeated, but Lacy was having none of Cassie's placating words.

"I saw it," Lacy said. "In a—"

"Book." They spoke the word in unison. *I saw it in a book* had become the refrain they'd spoken from the time they could read, and even before. Cassie had crystal clear memories of opening up picture books and seeing the images tell a story different than the one they were supposed to tell. She'd been only three years old when Maurice Sendak's Where the Wild Things Are had told her a different story than the one on the pages. The images of Max in his wolf costume, defying his mother and being sent to bed with no supper; Max having a wild rumpus with the Wild Things and being named king; Max returning to the safety of his home and his hot supper.

Even now, as she thought of it, the tears came because Cassie hadn't seen a hot supper still waiting for Max. Instead, the food had been cold, and she knew that meant her mother wouldn't always be there to keep her safe and warm and fed.

And then Annabel Lane had died, and that's when Cassie knew that books held a special power for her. A power she didn't want.

Cassie had tried one last time the night before. "Lacy. Listen to me," she'd placed her hands on her sister's shoulders. "Books aren't always right. We have to listen to ourselves. We can make our own destinies. We can change things."

But it was too late. Lacy shook herself free and stepped back. A wall had slammed down and Cassie knew there was nothing more she could say. Lacy believed their fate was written in stone.

Twenty-four hours later, Cassie left Cape Misery and Laurel Point behind.

Chapter 2

"It is not so difficult to be oneself."
~Rodney Barfield

"Why you headed to North Carolina?" the waitress asked.

Cassie had spent sleepless nights coming up with an answer to that question—one that didn't involve book magic. "The Outer Banks are supposed to be beautiful," she said. "I'm up for an adventure, so why not?"

In truth, books had given her the destination of Devil's Cove. Cassie had hated Aunt Rose's book magic teachings, but they were the one nonnegotiable Aunt Rose had. The girls had to learn the family gift. While Lacy had used fiction, Cassie had pulled the travel books from the shelves. She opened three different books, standing them on their spines and letting the sides fall. Three different books, and each time, they'd opened to pages about the Outer Banks.

So that was where she was headed. The books had

directed her. She'd tried to come up with other destinations in the country. She could go to California. It was close, after all, but the Golden State bordered the Pacific Ocean, just like Oregon did. She needed a bigger change than that.

She could go to Texas, or Wisconsin, or even New York. But none of these places sent the little burst of anticipation through her that the Outer Banks did.

She was going to make her own destiny, and in doing so, she'd listened to the book magic one last time before she cut it off for good.

Devil's Cove was her destination.

CASSIE HAD STUDIED the geography of Devil's Cove. She knew that to the east lay the barrier islands, and to the west was the mainland. Four ocean channels—Albermarle, Roanoke, Croatan, and Pamlico Sounds—flowed around the piece of land. Her little pickup truck bounced over the grates of the swing bridge that connected Sand Point to the island village of Devil's Cove. She drove around the island, taking in the brightly painted beach houses, the marinas, and the pier. The town was just as quaint as she'd imagined it would be, with its old storefronts, brick sidewalks, pots overflowing with flowers, and the cool breeze blowing off the sound. She held her breath, allowing herself to be in the moment and experience the feeling of peace spreading through her.

It was instant. This...Devil's Cove...was home.

Cassie had a list of things to accomplish, and a timeline during which to accomplish them. On her first day, she found a place to hang her hat. She's seen a flyer with little tear-offs stapled to a tree. Room for Rent. The woman with the vacancy in her house was named Hattie Juniper Pickle and lived on Rum Runner's Lane. Cassie had looked at the woman with her pink hair, leg warmers pooled around her ankles, and Madonna fingerless gloves and tried to hide her smile. Hattie had to be in her mid to late forties, but in her mind, she was clearly in her twenties. Or younger.

Fashion in the 80s had changed from the beginning of the decade. Gone were the Dittos bellbottom jeans and Farrah Fawcett hair, and in was the spiked punk look, big hair rock bands, and everything Madonna. Hattie Juniper Pickle had fully embraced the decade.

Cassie was more Stevie Nicks than Desperately Seeking Susan, but to each her own.

Her rented room at Hattie's house was colorful—four walls, four different colors (salmon, lavender, teal, and yellow)—but clean. It came with a bed, a dresser, a closet, and her own bathroom. That was all Cassie needed.

Her savings from her job at the Laurel Point Garden Center wouldn't last long, so on her second day, she located Bloom, the island's one and only nursery. They weren't hiring, but Cassie was dogged, throwing out the names of various flowers and shrubs, discussing zero scape yards, and even exploring the idea of fairy gardens.

In the end, Delilah Rose—wasn't that the most perfect name for someone who owned a garden center?—hired Cassie on the spot. "I don't need anyone right now, but I can't pass up a good thing."

Third on Cassie's To Do list was to find the library and bookstore. As it turned out, they were across the street from one another, at a diagonal, on Main Street. She couldn't avoid them all together, unfortunately, but she could as much as possible, and that was what mattered. Now that she knew where they were, she would be spending very little time on Main Street.

With each day that passed, Cassie felt more a part of Devil's Cove, and the hole in her heart, left from leaving Cape Misery, grew a tiny bit smaller. She longed to tell her parents about it—to sit on the bench or on a blanket in the little cemetery above the cape, filling them in on every detail of her new life.

She settled, instead, for starting a journal, filling page after page with her thoughts, dreams, and observations about life in the Southeast.

Chapter 3

"Sometimes nature guards her secrets with the unbreakable grip of physical law. Sometimes the true nature of reality beckons from just beyond the horizon."

~Brian Greene

*D*evil's Cove, it turned out, had its secrets, just like everyplace else in the world. Husbands cheated on wives. Wives cheated on husbands. The story of a teenager who'd run away a few years ago struck close to home for Cassie. She may have been nineteen when she left Laurel Point, but she'd still run away, hadn't she?

Shops were sometimes burglarized; women left their lives, leaving the island behind to strike out on their own, taking their children with them; boats disappeared at sea. For such a small village, the place had a million tales hidden beneath the surface.

Perry Hubbard's story was one of them. She was a recluse who lived in a stately old house across the street from Hattie. She took occasional walks, swinging a collapsed black umbrella like it was a cane, her posture rigid, her head held high as if a string connected the crown of her head to the clouds above. She didn't seem to have a schedule and Cassie could go weeks without seeing any trace of life in the house.

The woman never stepped foot in a store. If not for the weekly market delivery and the monthly yard maintenance provided by Bloom, Cassie might also have wondered if the old woman ever ate, or if, maybe, she was a ghost rather than a real, live living human. But she did get groceries, and she did arrange for her yard to be serviced, and once in a while Cassie saw her through one of the windows as she rattled around inside the house.

When an order came in for new flowers to be planted along the brick walkway leading the front porch of the place, Cassie begged Delilah to be the one to do the planting.

"Why are you so anxious to dig in the dirt there?" Delilah had asked her. She wore her blond hair back in a ponytail and had a Bloom Garden Center cap on, along with khaki shorts and a Bloom t-shirt. It was October, but unusually warm, so the shorts were still comfortable. Cassie wore the same outfit, only her shorts were denim. Her socks slouched inside her worn brown leather work boots and her gloves stuck halfway out of her back pocket.

The truth was, Cassie wanted to see inside the house, not that she thought she had a chance of that, but who knew. The old nursery rhyme came to her.

Old Mother Hubbard
Went to the Cupboard,

To give the poor Dog a bone;
When she came there,
The Cupboard was bare,
And so the poor Dog had none.

She went to the Bakers
To buy him some Bread;
When she came back
The Dog was dead!

She went to the Undertakers
To buy him a coffin;
When she came back
The Dog was laughing.

CASSIE NEVER DID UNDERSTAND that rhyme, but the image of a hunchbacked old woman with a kerchief on her head, tied under her chin, suddenly appearing at the door, a dog bone in hand came to mind. It was the exact opposite of the staunch posture and aloof nature of Perry Hubbard.

So many times Cassie had tried to work up the gumption to catch up to Mrs. Hubbard as she walked, but she never did. But today was the day, because today was planting day. Cassie pulled the curtain in her bedroom aside, staring at the beautiful old house across the street, imaging it with the flats of flowers in the bed of her truck already planted along both sides of the walkway. Empty pots sat at the base of the porch steps. Soon they'd be overflowing with flowers cascading down the sides.

Cassie was in love with the house's white clapboard siding, the black wrought iron fence, the wide wraparound porch. She could picture enclosing the left side of the porch with screening to make a sunroom. Rocking chairs. A family—

Her thoughts jerked to a halt. There had been several times when she'd walked by The Open Door Bookshop and she'd been so tempted to break her own rule, step inside, and use her book magic just to see what her future held. She stopped herself every time she got close to actually doing it. She'd made the decision to experience life as it was happening rather than using bibliomancy to prepare herself for the future, and she needed to stick to it, just like she needed to honor the vow she and Lacy had made to remain single and childless.

A black crow circled overhead. She watched it as it made another pass over the house before gliding away. It grew smaller and smaller, finally disappearing.

A sign to leave the past behind. She was trying.

She gazed longingly at the house once again. What she wouldn't give to live in a place like that. She was a minimalist, but growing up in the cramped, vertical lighthouse, then spending the last six months in this one room in Hattie's house made her crave space. The Mamas & the Papas song about dreaming came to mind, only her dreams were about the house on Rum Runner's Lane rather than California.

Cassie let the curtain fall back into place. She pulled her cap on, pulling her curly ponytail through the back hole, and headed out, literally making a U-turn in her truck and pulling up in front of Perry Hubbard's house two seconds later.

She'd heard the stories about the old Sea Captain who'd built it. He'd been a rum smuggler, escaping his ship before it descended into the Graveyard of the Atlantic. He'd come through the Inter-coastal Waterways on a shallop, and ended up in the island's sheltered inlet now called simply, the Cove.

The 17th century ship that had gone down had been carrying 'Devil's Rum', a liquor from the Caribbean. The name of the island came from that little bit of history and the luck of that sailor. Devil's Rum Cove became Devil's Cove, and the house over on the other side of the street from Hattie Juniper Pickle's had been built by that very seaman. Legend had it that he'd hidden away a treasure that had yet to be found. Rum? Gold? Nobody knew.

The old house, like most of the houses close to the water on the island, was built on a piling foundation meant to withstand the coastal elements of wind, water, and sand. Lattice across the base of the house blocked the gaping openness directly under the house itself, as well as the Sound beyond, but Cassie could smell the salt in the air. She felt a little bit giddy walking up the steps, pausing to look back across the street. From this vantage point, Hattie's house looked small, but still wildly colorful.

She turned back to face the screen door, taking a breath before pulling it open so she could knock on the door behind it.

No one came.

She waited, knocking again after thirty seconds had passed.

She thought she heard something from inside, but couldn't be sure. Still, no one came. She sighed, muttering to herself, "I had to try."

She had her instructions from Delilah. Take out the old plants, turn and amend the soil, then plant the flats of annuals, as well as more pampas grass along the left side of the house. There seemed to be plenty of pampas grass already, but Delilah said Mrs. Hubbard requested it, so she'd plant it. "Did she call you with the request?" Cassie had asked.

"Last week."

"What does she sound like?" Cassie asked, wondering if her voice would match the outward staunchness of her appearance.

If Delilah thought the question was strange, she didn't let on. "No nonsense. That woman doesn't suffer fools."

Now Cassie got to work, glancing up at the house every once in a while to see if there was any movement at any of the windows, but the place was as quiet as the Lane grave-yard back at the lighthouse. *Not a creature was stirring...*

"Ahoy there!"

The voice coming from the gate startled her. Cassie sat up on her knees, running the back of her hand across her forehead, then adjusting the bill of her cap back into place. A man stood at the fence, tipping his hat to her in a very old-fashioned way that made her smile. A boy who looked to be about nine or ten years old stood next to the man, his long arms dangling next to his beanpole body.

"Ahoy to you, too," she said.

"I've seen ya 'round the village. Wanted ta introduce myself. Salty Gallagher, at your service." He tugged at the boy's shirt so he stepped forward. "Boy, say hello."

The boy gave a little wave, then looked to the ground.

Cassie stood and walked up to them, peeling off her gloves. "Cassie Lane," she said.

Salty looked over her shoulder at the flowers she'd already planted along one side of the walkway. She was halfway done, and it was barely noon. She took a moment to study him. Tattoos ran up one arm, the main event being a bikini clad woman with a grass skirt. It felt like a throwback to another era, but here he was, older than her, but not by too many years, looking far too weathered for his age. The sun had done her due diligence with him, lining his face with premature wrinkles and a few sunspots. His hair was light and gingery, the sheen of his stubble contrasting his leathery skin.

"Lookin' good," Salty said, bringing his stormy grey eyes back to her, and she had an uncomfortable feeling he wasn't talking about the flowers.

"Thanks," she said.

"You're not from 'round here," he said.

Cassie wasn't well-versed enough to pinpoint where his accent was from, but she guessed it was Eastern Carolina, a hint of old cockney in it. She was learning.

"I'm from Oregon," she said.

"That's a long way off. What brought ya here?"

He seemed genuinely interested. Maybe she was judging him too harshly. She glanced back at the flats of flowers on the walkway. "You know, fresh start and all that," she said. Her aching for Lacy and Aunt Rose and her parents was fading, but not enough to prevent the pricking behind her eyelids. "It, um, seemed like as good a place as any."

"Better, I reckon'." Salty gave another tip of his cap. "Devil's Cove welcomes ya."

She smiled, pointedly glancing back at the flats of flowers laid out on the bricks. "I better get back now. Nice meeting you, Salty."

She nodded to the sullen boy.

Salty's grin spread under his bulbous nose. "I'll see ya 'round, Cassie Lane."

She smiled, but inside she hoped she didn't see him around too often. Something about Salty Gallagher struck her as odd.

Chapter 4

"The dead keep their secrets."
~Alexander Smith

*W*hile Cassie was finishing up, a boxy army green SUV bumped along Rum Runner's Lane. She glanced up to see it stopped at the three way a block down. A moment later, it bounced along the road, coming to a stop right in front of Perry Hubbard's house. A man jumped out, slamming the driver's side door with a loud bang. He took two brown paper grocery sacks from the back, managed to hold them with one hand while he unlatched the gate, and strode in. He had a slim pair of silver headphones on, small gray pads resting against his ears, and a Walkman clipped to the waistband of his jeans.

He registered Cassie near the flowerbeds, but didn't make eye contact.

Cassie raised a gloved hand in a wave. "Hey," she said.

The man slowed, readjusted the bags to one hand again,

and flipped the headphones off his head, leaving them cradling his neck. "Hey. Groceries," he said, lifting the bags slightly to prove he did, in fact, have groceries. His dark curly hair was cut short and he wore mirrored aviators. The guy clearly thought he was *all that*, but Cassie raised a brow. He had to be in his late twenties. In her book, delivering groceries as you headed into your thirties wasn't that cool. Then again, he had a workman's hands, rough and cut up, so maybe he was doing this as a side gig in between construction jobs.

She was being too judgmental. Lacy always called her out on that. She shook those thoughts away and jumped up. Surely Mrs. Hubbard would answer the door for her groceries. "Need some help?" she asked, but the man shook his head.

She gestured to the flower beds. "Planting flowers for Mrs. Hubbard."

He held up the bags again. "Sadler's."

You had to cross the bridge to the mainland to go to one of the larger supermarket chains. Most locals preferred Sadler's Market, Cassie, and apparently Mrs. Hubbard, included.

"Sure I can't help you?"

The man moved forward again. "Nope."

She watched as he took the steps two at a time. He opened the screen door, holding it with his back as he knocked. Almost instantly, the door opened.

Cassie hoped to catch Perry Hubbard's eye. Maybe get a little wave. Just an acknowledgement that would create the opportunity for another conversation some other time. And maybe a tour of the old house. She craned her neck to see, but the man from Sadler's was in the way, blocking her view of Mrs. Hubbard.

She heard the low murmur of their voices as they spoke. A second later, the door closed. The delivery man let the screen door slam shut. He put his headphones back on, plowed past Cassie without a glance, and in seconds flat, he was back in his car and driving away.

Cassie looked back at the house. She could offer put the groceries away for her, but she dismissed that idea right away. She couldn't force her way into the woman's life. She kept to herself, and that was just the way it was. It seemed like such a lonely existence. Cassie missed her sister and aunt like crazy. The aching hole in her heart had filled and softened around the edges with each passing day, but it would never go away. She longed for connections with people, and here Perry Hubbard was, shutting everyone out.

The house was completely still again. No sign of life.

As she climbed into her truck, another vehicle pulled up in front of the house. A young man, maybe in his late teens...close to Cassie's age, got out, went through the gate, and walked up the porch, a small white bag in his hand. He rang the doorbell, but instead of waiting, he opened the screen door and set the bag down, letting it close again, the bag nestled between the two doors.

A second later, the front door opened, Mrs. Hubbard crouched down to retrieve the delivery, and once again, she disappeared inside.

She was a strange bird, there was no doubt about that.

CASSIE SPENT the late afternoon losing herself in the plants at the garden center, helping people decide what to plant in the fall months, but most of the conversations turned to a woman who'd vanished the day before. Faith Dresher. A neighbor hadn't seen her for days, grew worried, and reported her missing after she'd asked the husband about her and he'd acted suspicious. The sheriff had shown up to find that the neighbor had been right. Faith Dresher was not at home, but her husband had told the authorities she'd needed a break and had gone to visit family.

The people of Devil's Cove didn't believe it.

"The sheriff believed that? Pfft."

"Without her baby? No way."

"I bet he killed her."

"Right. It's always the husband."

"Poor thing."

People talked like the woman was dead, but Cassie didn't want to believe that. Maybe she'd just run away. Maybe she'd just wanted a chance at a new life, like Cassie had, even if it meant leaving her baby behind.

Still, something about the missing woman bothered her. Cassie had read the newspaper article in the day's edition of the Devil's Cove Gazette. There was a grainy photograph of a twenty-something pregnant woman. The man next to her had his arm draped around her shoulder.

Cassie thought back to more of the gossip she'd heard at Bloom.

How could she leave her child?

Heartless.

Mark my words, he stashed her body somewhere.

He's guilty as sin.

People were certainly quick to place blame.

Now, back at home for the night, Cassie didn't want to be alone in her room. She followed the ribbon of cigarette smoke out to the front porch. Hattie sat against the pale green exterior of her house, staring into space. Cassie pulled the other Adirondack chair alongside her, avoiding the less comfortable aluminum-framed patio chair with the wide rubber strips crisscrossing across the back and seat. "Those things'll kill you," she said.

Hattie tapped her cigarette, the cylinder of ash falling into the ashtray next to her in response.

"I can't stop thinking about that woman," Cassie said.

"Why's that? Do you know her?"

"No, but I don't have to know her to be worried for her. She's missing. She left her child. There has to be a good reason for her to have done that."

The breeze shifted. The smoke from the cigarette dangling from Hattie's lips curled up into her eyes. Still, she left the cigarette between her lips and picked absently at her fingernails. "People got their secrets."

That was true, but it felt like a weighted idea. Secrets could be full of hope, despair, and a million other emotions. What secrets did Faith Dresher hold close to her chest? Cassie told Hattie some of the gossip and speculation she'd heard. "Do you think something happened to her, or do you think she left on her own?"

Hattie finally took the cigarette from her mouth and rubbed it out in the ashtray. She turned to face Cassie, looking far more serious than Cassie had ever seen her. Hattie's smile was usually ever-present, but now she wore a deep frown. "That I don't know."

Chapter 5

"Love is the longing for the half of ourselves we have lost."
~Milan Kundera, *The Unbearable Lightness of Being*

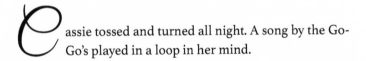assie tossed and turned all night. A song by the Go-Go's played in a loop in her mind.

> Can you hear them?
> They talk about us
> Telling lies
> Well, that's no surprise

Who was talking? Who was telling lies? Why in the world was that song stuck in her head?

Too many questions.

Her eyes were bloodshot, and she ached for sleep, but it

was elusive. Finally, she gave up trying, got dressed, and plaited her hair, the braid hanging down the center of her back. She tiptoed through the house, leaving but with no destination in mind.

By the time she'd made it to the point where Rum Runner's Lane turned into Main Street, she realized it was too chilly for the white gauzy dress she'd put on. A cold front was coming in. She should have grabbed a sweater, but she didn't want to turn back now. The walk would warm her up.

Cassie kept her eyes straight ahead as she passed the old buildings whose backs were to the beach; past the bookstore on her left and the library on her right; past the long fishing pier that stretched like a finger over the water. She came to two of the island's marinas, passing Dolphin's Landing first, then Devil's Cove Landing. The fish market was next. She'd spent the last six months getting to know all the island village's nooks and crannies, but the fish market was a place she hadn't yet visited.

It opened early and closed early. Fishermen were out on their boats before the crack of dawn, and often docked again before some of the village businesses had even opened for the day. The strong scent of fish hung in the air inside the building.

The fish mongers worked with the restaurant owners who showed up early to get the fresh catch of the day and with the locals who came for the same reason. Cassie hadn't come for fish. She'd ended up here by happenstance, trying to get her mind off the missing mother.

It worked for a few minutes. She drew in the energy of the market, smiling despite her worries. She made it to the end of the building. Turning to head back the other way, she locked eyes with a young man who looked like he'd just gotten off a boat from a morning of fishing. Which, she realized, he probably had. His orange jacket had Raglan sleeves with reflective stripes on the shoulder, and a hood that was pushed back, revealing the man's mussed hair falling over his forehead. He held the handle of a bucket with one hand, and had something tucked under the opposite arm.

He smiled at her, an impish grin that lit up his whole face. Bright blue eyes edged with crow's feet. Squared off sideburns. The guy was a lookalike for Robert Redford in Butch Cassidy and the Sundance Kid, his hair a darker shade of blond, and minus the mustache.

An invisible strand of energy flowed between them, holding Cassie in place as if she were caught by a lightning bolt. She suddenly felt as if she was the only person in the fish market.

"Cassie?"

She heard someone calling her name.

"Cassie Lane, is that you?"

This time, she reacted, spinning around, breaking the connection with the fisherman, and running smack into another seafaring sailor, this one wearing a brown corduroy cap and rubber fishing pants. That bulbous nose. That hula girl tattoo. Salty Gallagher.

She deflated. She wanted to turn back around, renew the connection with the mystery man in the orange jacket, but instead she said good morning to Salty. Aunt Rose didn't raise her to be rude.

"What brings ya to the fish mart so early in the mornin'?" Salty asked, looking totally oblivious to Cassie's distracted mind.

"Just out walking," she said. "My feet led me here."

"You're an early riser, eh?" He flicked his bushy eyebrows

up to his forehead and one side of his mouth lifted in a knowing grin, as if her morning habits were illicit somehow.

"Today I was. I feel like--" She pressed the flat of her palm to her stomach, the coiled nerves loosening. "Something's off, but I don't know what."

Salty gave her a knowing look. "Bit o' the sixth sense, eh?"

No, her only gift was bibliomancy. Still, she couldn't shake the feeling deep in her gut.

The fish market suddenly felt stifling. Growing up by the sea meant there'd never been a shortage of fresh air, and that's what she needed now. "I have to go," she said. "Good seeing you, Salty."

He doffed his cap. "'Till next time," he said with a wink that sent a niggling bit of unease down her spine. There was something about Salty Gallagher that she didn't quite trust.

She turned, hoping to catch another glimpse of the man with the impish grin, but while there were several of the same or similar bright orange jackets moving around the fish market, none of them belonged to the fisherman who'd caught her eye.

It was probably better that way.

She gave Salty another wave, feeling his eyes on her as she walked toward the exit door. She left without a backwards glance, sure she wouldn't see the man she wanted to, and equally sure she would see Salty still staring at her.

She started to retrace her steps, heading toward the marinas and the fishing pier. Her eyes locked on something on the ground ahead of her. As she came closer, she saw it was a book, opened up to a random page. She started to sidestep around it, but just like the magnetic draw she'd felt with the man inside the fish market, the words of the book seemed to undulate and lift off the page, calling her.

"I don't do books," she murmured under her breath, as if the book itself would hear her, but try as she might to get her feet to keep moving, she was rooted in place. The book was summoning her.

She crouched down and touched either side of the book's covers, ready to simply slam it shut, but a breeze swirled and the open pages fluttered, turning back and forth until they settled again on a new page.

A page just for her.

Cassie gulped. Blinked. She hadn't sought out this book; the book had, it seemed, sought out *her*.

"Okay," she said, and she looked at the open pages. The words swelled and rippled, one line growing darker and seeming to peel away from the empty space beneath them.

"A person who longs to leave the place where he lives is an unhappy person."

SHE FELT her heart stop for a beat. She'd left Laurel Point, but she never would have said she was unhappy. Unfulfilled was a better way to put it. And determined to make her own destiny.

"Are you okay?"

A man's voice carved its way into her thoughts. She blinked. Looked at the book again. The letters had resettled onto the page, forming ordinary words with no magical powers. "I am," she said, flipping the book closed as she stood up.

Only then did she look up and straight into the bright blue eyes of the man she'd seen inside the fish market.

Those eyes that sent her mind reeling back to the blue skies above the lighthouse at Cape Misery and Laurel Point. Those cerulean skies, dotted with puffs of clouds, expanding toward the horizon.

The book in her hands grew warm to the touch. She wobbled on her feet as the image of a woman flashed in her mind. Cassie was not overcome with this man, as inexplicably drawn to him as she was. She looked down at the book she held, and something became very clear. The message about leaving a place—it wasn't about her.

She felt the color drain from her face. Who *was* it about, then?

He took her arm, steadying her. "Are you sure you're all right?"

She breathed in, the air fortifying her. "Yep. Positive. I just...someone dropped this--"

"I did. I was retracing my steps to look for it."

She glanced down at the book's jacket. On it, two arms stretching up, either catching or tossing a bowler hat. "Have you read it?" the man asked.

He'd released her arm, the spot where he'd touched suddenly cold compared to the rest of her. "No," she said, handing it to him, but a ribbon of cold wound its way through her body as she registered the title. *The Unbearable Lightness of Being*. It was the same book Lacy had found outside the door of Books by Bequest.

"It's about a man who cheats, but at the same time is in love with his girlfriend."

She made a sound—something between a disapproving grunt and a noncommittal, "Hmmph." The book had told Lacy that Cassie would betray her, but a story about an adulterous man certainly had nothing to do with her.

He smiled at that. "Yeah." He tucked the book back

under his arm, extending his other out to her. "Leo Hawthorne."

She was overcome with the desire to move her fingertips to his bangs and brush them to the side. He needed a haircut. Instead, she took his hand. "Cassandra Lane."

"Ah, sweet Cassandra. Are you cursed?"

She started. "W-What?"

"Like your namesake, the Trojan princess with the gift of prophecy, courtesy of Apollo, then cursed by him so nobody would believe her."

The meaning of her name. Of course. She'd never understood why her parents had chosen to name her Cassandra. Growing up, she'd longed for something light and lovely, like Lacy. Instead she was burdened with a name that was a constant reminder of her bibliomancy...and the weight of the curse.

"I go by Cassie," she said, finally placing her hand in his.

He nodded, then walked with her past the marinas. They made their way down the pier, past the benches where the serious early fishermen and women cast their lines from, past the large square galvanized steel sink, and to the end. They leaned against the railing, forearms resting on the damp wood. A shiver passed over her skin. Instantly, as if Leo Hawthorne sensed her chill, he laid his book on the bench behind them, shrugged out of his lined jacket, and draped it over her shoulders. The scent of him lingered on the jacket—a mix of saltwater and fish—not something she'd normally find appealing, but...well, she did.

He'd walked her all the way to the end of Main Street before it turned in to Rum Runner's Lane. "Nice to meet you, Cassandra," he'd said, her name falling easily from his lips.

Later at work, as she held the hose, letting a light spray

of water shower the plants at the garden center, she thought of the many reasons to stay away from Leo Hawthorne. First, he was a fisherman, and the Lane curse said that the men would be taken by the sea. She reasoned that anyone she was with wouldn't actually *be* a Lane. Then again, though, neither was her mother. She'd been a Lane only by marriage, but the curse had taken her.

Second, he'd had that book with him. Five seconds with it, and it had presented her with a message. She couldn't be faced with that constantly.

And third, Cassie was not going to bear children, so she planned to steer clear of men altogether. No relationships meant no marriage, which meant no possibility of children. Surely Leo Hawthorne wanted a family one day. That would seal the deal. There was no future between them. Cassie had to stay away from him.

Later that night, she wrote in her journal, not about Leo, but about the message the book had given her.

"A person who longs to leave the place where he lives is an unhappy person."

A NIGGLING FEELING that sat like a stone in the pit of her stomach. *The Unbearable Lightness of Being* had told Lacy that Cassie would betray her. Had it been about Leo Hawthorne? Was he the betrayal her sister had foreseen?

Chapter 6

"I have gone to this bookshop for years, always finding the one book I wanted - and then three more I hadn't known I wanted."
   ~Mary Ann Shaffer, *The Guernsey Literary and Potato Peel Pie Society*

*C*assie stood smack in the middle of the street, looking to her right at the pale blue converted house that was Devil's Cove Library, then to her left at The Open Door, the village bookshop. Both were places she swore never to step foot in, but this morning, she was breaking her own rule. The question was, which one was she going to enter?

The question was answered for her when a man appeared at the open door of the bookshop, beckoning. He was overdressed for an island on the Outer Banks, but he seemed utterly comfortable in his belted dark grey slacks, white button-down shirt, sleeves folded halfway up the forearms, and narrow black tie.

"Come," he said in a deep baritone.

She placed a palm to her chest as she looked over her shoulder. "Me?"

He chuckled, warm and welcoming. "Yes, you. You look undecided, so I thought I would make the decision for you. You can visit the library another time, yes?"

Cassie hadn't realized she'd been that obvious. She walked to the sidewalk, pausing in the threshold of the store. Instantly, she was overcome with curiosity. Books had never spoken to her like they did Lacy, but the scent of books, old and new, drew her in even when she fought against it. She'd realized early on that there was a big difference between being indifferent to books and being a conscientious objector of her family's curse. She didn't want books to control her life, or predict her future, but she missed the stories written on the pages.

Those stories propelled her feet forward.

The Open Door was vastly different than Books by Bequest back in Laurel Point. Both spaces had book-filled shelves lining the walls, but here, freestanding shelves ran up and down the center of the room, as well. She breathed in the musty smell of well-used books, well-worn paper, and well-loved stories.

The immediate difference between Books by Bequest and The Open Door was that the latter focused just as much on new books as it did on old. The Lane's bookstore, by comparison, was sustained primarily by its robust mail order business. People were always on the hunt for hard to find and out of print books, and that had become Books by Bequest's specialty.

At the lighthouse, tables in the center of the shop held stacks and stacks of books. It was a wonder Aunt Rose knew where anything was, but she did. It was a mess, but it was her mess. Anytime Cassie had tried to straighten things up, she'd gotten a scolding. "I know where everything is. Don't change it."

Here, things were tidy. From what she could see, everything had a place, and everything was in its place. The service counter in the center of the room was created by four counters which created a rectangle with a single passthrough through which the store clerk could enter. A double-sided shelf was in the middle of the checkout space. Books were banded, last names written on sheets of paper wrapped about the different books. Special orders, she knew. Wax coated bookmarks were organized in a tray, little tassels hanging from the tops of them. Other than that, the place was all books. No mugs, or games, or stationary products.

The used book section was in the back of the store, a hand-painted sign hanging on the brick wall above those shelves. The new books filled the rest of the shelves, with end caps and displays highlighting the hot new releases.

The new books didn't speak to Cassie as much as the old books did. It was the same for Lacy and Aunt Rose. New books didn't have stories to tell beyond the words themselves. They felt hollow compared to books that had been held, read, loved.

Cassie wasn't as well-practiced as her sister, but she knew that if she wanted to use her bibliomancy, the best bet was to use books that had been held by someone's hands. Words, after all, could be interpreted in different ways by different people. Those interpretations were absorbed into the pages, and those books had more to communicate. It didn't matter what size the books were, or what shade of the rainbow the cover was. If she placed a book on its spine and let it fall open, it would reveal something to her. They held worlds like the one in *The Unbearable Lightness of Being* that Leo Hawthorne had dropped the day before. They held the stories written by authors, but they also conveyed hidden stories that only a bibliomancer could read.

These messages were what she usually sought to avoid.

"Come," the man said again. He wore the ghost of a smile, as if he knew something about Cassie and her connection to books, which, of course, was impossible. The truth was, to him, she was just an indecisive woman. "What can I help you with?"

She'd come to buy her own copy of *The Unbearable Lightness of Being*. The fact that Lacy had a copy, which had foretold Cassie's betrayal, and that Leo Hawthorne had a copy, which had spooked her beyond belief, meant that book was important and might have something else to tell her.

Before she could hunt down the area of the store where Milan Kundera's book was housed, her eyes fell upon a stack of hardcover books. *Not Without My Daughter: A True Story.* The title was written in dark red, turning even darker under her gaze.

"Ah," the bookseller said, following her gaze. "An astonishing tale. Brand new."

She read the copy on the cream cover.

She was an American trapped in Tehran — Imprisoned by her husband. The underground said they could get her out, but she would have to leave her little girl behind...

"It's quite a compelling read." The man picked up a copy and held it out to her. Cassie wanted to stretch her arm out. To take hold of the book. To see what it had to tell her. Instead, she took a step backward.

He angled his head, looking at her curiously. "Ah, a woman who knows what she doesn't want."

That wasn't entirely true, though, was it? Because that book was precisely what Cassie wanted. She just hadn't known it before she'd come into the store.

"Not Without My Daughter." She muttered the title under her breath and inched closer to the bookseller. "Not Without My Daughter," she said again, and then, without thinking, she held her hand out.

He released the book to her and she read what it was about.

In August 1984, Michigan housewife Betty Mahmoody accompanied her husband to his native Iran for a two-week vacation that turned into a permanent stay. To her horror, she found herself and her four-year-old daughter, Mahtob, virtual prisoners of a man rededicated to his Shiite Muslim faith, in a land where women are near-slaves and Americans despised. Their only hope for escape lay in a dangerous underground that would not take her child.

In Cassie's experience, bibliomancy didn't mean books called to her. It didn't mean she was drawn to choose a specific book that would tell her something. At least it never had operated that way before. She'd come in for one book, but she knew now that this book by Betty Mahmoody was the one she needed.

She looked around. "Can I sit somewhere? To look at it?"

The bookseller's eyes narrowed for a moment, and she knew he was wondering what was going on inside her head. If only she could tell him. If only she could tell *someone*, but besides Hattie Juniper Pickle, who seemed a little halfcocked all the time, and Delilah Rose at Bloom, there was no one Cassie could talk to, and no matter what, she couldn't tell either of them about her being a bibliomancer. She wanted to fit in. Telling people she had a divination wasn't the way to be normal.

What she needed to do, she realized with a start, was call Lacy.

"Never mind," she said, making a split-second decision. "I'll take this one." She walked to the check out counter where he met her on the other side.

"A woman who knows what she wants, after all," he said with a bemused smile.

Cassie smiled back as she handed him a twenty-dollar bill. "Looks like—" What had he said? Ah yes— "a compelling read."

"You'll let me know what you think of it, won't you?" He handed her a business card. White heavy stock. A simple font in black.

The Open Door Bookshop
Cyrus McAdams, Proprietor

"I will, Mr. McAdams," she said.

He slipped the hardcover book, along with a hand-written receipt, into a thin bag stamped with the bookshop's name.

As she left, she felt his gaze on her, but it didn't feel the same as when Salty Gallagher's eyes followed her. There was nothing discomfiting lurking behind his attention. No, interestingly, she felt reassured, almost as if he could help her in some way.

BACK IN HER room at Hattie's, Cassie sat cross-legged on her bed, the unopened book in front of her. Her nerve-endings flared, feeling like live wires touching each other, igniting sparks. She was torn. On the one hand, she didn't want to put the book on its spine and let it fall open. She didn't want to see what message the words inside had to tell her. She didn't want to try to *interpret* those words. What if she was wrong?

On the other hand, how could she *not* do it? Because she knew the book had something to tell her about Faith Dresher.

She couldn't quite bring herself to call Lacy. She longed to hear her sister's voice, but she didn't have the energy to fight with her. She decided to wait until later when she had less on her mind.

She drew in a deep inhalation before she set the copy of *Not Without My Daughter* on its spine, holding on to either side of the cover.

Aunt Rose hadn't been persnickety about the method she and Lacy used to tap into their bibliomancy.

They could close their eyes or keep them open wide.

They could ask their question—for that's what they had

to do, ask a question—aloud...or silently inside their heart. Either way worked.

They could put their finger down on the page, or they could wait for some sentence or phrase, or even a single word to riffle or peel off the page.

Cassie closed her eyes, drawing in another deep breath to tamp down her beating heart. It had been close to a year since she'd picked up a book, let alone practiced any book magic. She had a fleeting thought that maybe she no longer had the ability.

She expelled the air trapped in her lungs as she thought about Faith Dresher, and then the question came to her in a thought. *Is she safe?*

She released the sides of the book, letting it fall open. She opened her eyes, instantly seeing the boldface words on the page.

"Were Mahtob and I prisoners? Hostages? Captives of this venomous stranger who had once been a loving husband and father?"

Chapter 7

*"Remember happiness doesn't depend upon who you are or
what you have; it depends solely on what you think."*
~Dale Carnegie

Cassie awoke with a fierce determination to help
Faith Dresher. She just didn't know how to do that.
The woman could have left Devil's Cove, disappearing
somewhere on the vast mainland—which was the United
States.

She could be in hiding right here on the island.

Or, like the gossipers she'd overheard at Bloom, she
could be dead.

In the kitchen, she headed straight for the coffeepot.
Hattie had an eclectic collection of mugs. This morning,
Cassie selected a white campfire mug with the village's logo
in sea green—an anchor inside a circle with the town's
name. The two Vs in Devil's Cove touched the points of the
anchor.

"She's back."

Hattie's raspy voice startled Cassie. Her arm jerked and the coffee splashed over the edge of the mug. She spun around, coffeepot in one hand, tin cup in the other, to see Hattie standing in front of the bright teal refrigerator, an orange in one hand. "Who's back?"

Holding onto the orange, Hattie scratched the top of her head with her index finger. "That missing woman. She came back."

Cassie shoved the coffeepot back into place and set down her half-filled mug. She felt as if the anchor that had been yanking her heart down into the pit of her stomach had been freed, lightening her load and setting things right. "Oh my God, that's great!"

Hattie moved to the counter and began peeling the orange. She tossed bits of peel over her shoulder where they landed on the square tiles. "Is it, though?"

"Why wouldn't it be?"

Hattie held a section of her orange between her fingers, wagging it at Cassie. "You planted that seed in my head. I have plenty to think about with my love life, you know. Mr. Pickle and me, we're gettin' close again. I think we're gonna mosey down the wedding aisle again. But *you* were worried about that woman, and now *I'm* worried about her, too. "Why'd she left in the first place. Not only that, but leaving her baby behind."

The warm relief that had flooded Cassie turned cold. The passage from the book shot into her head. There was more to Faith's story, of that she was certain.

∾

CASSIE SPENT the day at the garden center rearranging the plants and giving them a light water. The island was expecting rain in the next day or two, so there was no need to oversaturate.

She listened to the gossip, and found that people still had plenty to say about Faith Dresher.

"He drove her to it."

"He's probably abusive."

"She never comes out of that house."

"He probably keeps her trapped. That's probably what drove her to escape."

"But she left her baby."

"I guess we'll never know."

Cassie thought about that last question and wondered, why not? Maybe Faith Dresher needed someone to talk to— just like Cassie did.

The bottom line was, she couldn't ignore what the book had told her. Now that she'd opened that can of worms, she was stuck dealing with them. She decided then and there to pay a visit to Faith Dresher. She could be this woman's friend. Or at least she could try.

She'd looked up Faith's name in the white pages. She wasn't listed, but there was a Dresher. A man named Carl who lived on Magpie Lane.

It was worth a shot.

At the end of her shift, Cassie climbed into her truck and started the engine. Delilah caught up with her just before she pulled out of the gravel parking lot. Cassie rolled down the window and crooked her arm on the frame.

Delilah wore a smile nearly one hundred percent of the time, but right now, her mouth pulled into a frown and two vertical lines were carved into the space between her brows. "Everything okay?" Cassie asked.

"I don't know. You were at old Mrs. Hubbard's the other day, right?"

"Right. Planting the beds along the front walkway."

"Did you happen to see her?"

"Yes and no. She didn't answer when I knocked, but she answered the door to get her groceries."

Delilah clasped the bill of her garden center cap and readjusted it. Her frown deepened. "I haven't gotten a check from her for the mulching we did last month. She's persnickety with everything, including paying her bills. I called, but there was no answer."

"Maybe it's lost in the mail?" Cassie suggested.

Delilah pressed her fingers to her lips. "Maybe. I'm not worried about the bill. I'm worried about *her*. But if you saw her..."

She trailed off, leaving some unspoken question in the air between them.

The house across the street was always silent, but had it been more silent than usual? Were there degrees of silence? Cassie couldn't answer that. She hadn't seen any sign of Mrs. Hubbard since she'd planted the flowers, but that wasn't unusual. Still, maybe it was worth checking out. The woman was elderly. "Should you call the sheriff to, I don't know, check in on her?"

Delilah looked to the sky. Her chest rose and fell with a heavy breath. "I'll try to call her again first. It's just...if something's happened to her..."

She turned to head back to the office. "Let me know?" Cassie called.

Delilah waved without looking back.

Cassie put Perry Hubbard into a compartment in her mind. She'd think about her after she'd paid her visit to Faith Dresher.

Ten minutes later, she drove through the tidy residential neighborhood and turned onto Magpie Lane. Carl Dresher's little redbrick house had a single peaked roof with a smaller peak covering the equally small front porch. The house was a square, with an empty carport on the right side. The front yard was a square of grass with no walkway leading to the door. Cassie parked her truck along the sidewalk and walked through the splotchy grass and up the two brick steps. She knocked on the side of the white screen door and stepped back to the edge of the porch.

Nobody came.

She knocked again, cocking her ear to listen for signs of life.

Finally, after her third try, the door cracked open and a man peered out. "Help you?" he asked, his Carolina accent light, but there.

Cassie wanted to get a better look at him, but the details of his face were hidden behind the screening. "My name's Cassie. I'm looking for Faith?"

His lips pursed at the sound of a baby crying. "She's busy."

"I can wait."

"She's busy," he repeated.

Cassie had wondered if seeing Faith Dresher would be as simple as knocking on the door. Now she knew it wouldn't. She took out one of Bloom's business cards she'd brought with her, her name and Hattie's phone number scrawled on the back. "Okay, well, if you could give her this? She, um, entered a contest for a garden makeover." The man just stared, so Cassie added, "She won!"

She'd made up the story on the fly, pretty sure saying she was here to check on the wellbeing of his wife wasn't going to fly with this guy.

He slipped his hand out and snatched the card from her, then with a grunt, he closed the door.

And that, as they say, was that.

She went back to her truck by way of the driveway, glancing back through the chain link fence into the backyard. Weeds choked the brick walkway leading to an aluminum-roofed outbuilding that looked halfway collapsed. A dead bunch of pampas grass, which was pretty hard to kill, needed to be yanked out. The Dresher's yard could certainly use a makeover. Cassie's imagination went to work. In it, she tore down that outbuilding, added pavers and a fountain, flower beds in the corners, and a picket fence instead of the chain link.

She walked down the driveway, sending a backwards glance at the receding house. She knew from her own experience that leaving what you knew wasn't easy. This was a depressing place, true, but something else had to have driven Faith away from her home. The coil of nerves in her gut tightened as the line from Leo Hawthorne's book circled in her mind.

"A person who longs to leave the place where he lives is an unhappy person."

THE QUOTE from Not Without My Daughter was quick on its heels. The woman was unhappy and trapped.

What's making you so unhappy, Faith?

Chapter 8

"It strikes me profoundly that the world is more often than not a bad and cruel place."

~Bret Easton Ellis, *American Psycho*

Cassie didn't have time to ponder Faith's life once she got back to Hattie's rainbow house. She called Delilah to see if she'd heard anything about Mrs. Hubbard across the street. "Better safe than sorry," she said, "so I called the Sheriff's Department. They said they had a message from her grandson a few days ago that they were going out of town and asked if they could they do a drive-by once or twice."

That explained it. "I'm sure she just forgot to mail the check before she left," Cassie said.

Delilah let out a relieved sigh. "Yeah. I'll catch up with her when she gets back."

Cassie replaced the pink handset back in its cradle, running her hand over the twisted spiraled cord. It needed unwinding, but she'd do that later. She made herself a cup of tea, blowing the steam away as she sat at the table, thinking.

Hattie came into the kitchen, her gray kitty on her heels, meowing. Hattie crouched and scooped a little kibble from the Tupperware container sitting on the floor and poured it into the cat's bowl.

Cassie leaned back in her chair, watching as Cucumber (a nod to Hattie's last name of Pickle) rubbed up against Hattie's leg, waiting for her to get out of the way. "Where does Mrs. Hubbard's grandson live?" Cassie asked.

Hattie moved the bowl toward Cucumber with her purple-clogged foot. "What in the world are you talking about?"

"Perry Hubbard's grandson called the sheriff to ask them to keep an eye on her house. Said they'd be out of town for a little while. I was just wondering where he lives. I mean, when you live in a vacation spot right on the water, where do you go for vacation?" she asked, the irony of her escaping her own coastal home not lost on her.

Hattie drew her head back sharply. "Perry Hubbard doesn't have a grandson. Or any family. The Hubbard line dies out with her, just like the Juniper Pickle line dies with me." She waggled her head with attitude. "We are the single ladies in town—at least until I get hitched again. Perry's been alone ever since she moved into that house. I asked her once—before she became the recluse she is now, 'course—why she wanted to rattle around in that big ol' place by herself. She just shrugged and said, why not? So that's what she's been doing all these years...rattlin' around."

Cassie's brain had hitched on Hattie's first statement: *Perry Hubbard doesn't have a grandson.*

"I think the loneliness finally got to her 'bout ten years

ago—" Hattie was saying, her gaze on her fingers and the cuticle she was picking at—"'cause that's 'bout when she stopped coming outside. She used to plant the flowers along the front walkway herself, and she used to go to the market, too. She used to do a lot of things that she doesn't—"

"Hattie," Cassie interrupted, a sharpness in her tone.

Hattie's head snapped up.

"Someone at the Sheriff's Department said Perry Hubbard's *grandson* called them. To say they'd be out of town."

Hattie's bright pink lips arched downward into a heavy frown, registering what that meant. "That can't be right. She doesn't have a grandson," she repeated.

Cassie's feet moved before she'd even formulated the action in her mind. She was out of the kitchen, through the living room, and halfway down the porch steps when Hattie's clogs clacked against the floor behind her and her shrill voice said, "Do you think something's happened to her?"

Cassie couldn't answer that, but if she believed the feeling deep in her gut, then the answer was yes. "If there's no grandson, then possibly. Yes."

"What's the plan?" Hattie pressed. "If she doesn't answer, we should just go on in, right? Even if we have to bust the door...down. We can do it. I might not look it...but I'm strong." Hattie prattled on, muttering something about Perry Hubbard's house key and taking gulps of air in between, her blackened lungs impeding her fluid chatter. "If I was trapped..." Gasp. "...or on the floor..." Gasp. "...in my house...hurt...s...s...someone better break down..." Gasp. "...break down...the door. You hear me...Cassie?" Gasp. "You have my permission...to break...down...my...door."

"Those cigarettes'll kill you before anything else does," Cassie said over her shoulder. She'd wore jeans, a pair of lemon yellow lace-up Keds, and a lemon eyelet top, and she'd grabbed her thin navy sweater from the chair by the front door as she'd barreled outside, shrugging into it to ward off the chill. Now she pulled it tight, less against the cooling evening temperature than the foreboding feeling hovering just under her skin. "If we're worried about her, it won't be breaking and entering, will it? We're concerned neighbors."

She'd asked the question to herself, echoing what Hattie had asked a minute ago. This time Hattie offered reassurance. "We can't worry...'bout that. If a woman is in trouble, it's up to us to...help her." Hattie picked up speed and took hold of Cassie's arm, pulling her with her.

They kept on, finally lifting the lever of the black iron gate. They let it bang closed behind them as they hurried up the brick walkway, the colors of the flowers Cassie had planted diffused in the gloaming.

The porch steps were wide enough that they could climb them side-by-side. Hattie sucked in ragged breaths of air, but before Cassie could do it, she'd steadied herself and yanked open the screen door, hammering her fist on the interior door and hollering, "Perry Hubbard! Open this door. Perry!"

No answer.

Hattie opened her hand, slapping her palm against the door this time.

Still nothing.

Cassie grabbed hold of the doorknob. It was loose in her grip. She tried to turn it. It rattled, but was firmly locked.

She looked at Hattie and shook her head.

"Perry Hubbard!" Hattie's voice was loud on a normal day. When she raised it to a yell—and right at Cassie's ear—it was deafening. "Open up!"

They both turned their heads, angling their ears toward the door. Cassie listened for any trace of sound. For a second, she thought she heard something. She leaned closer, her back against the screen door, holding it open.

Silence.

"Perry Hubbard!" Hattie hollered again, even louder this time. "Are you in there? Open this door!"

"Let's check the windows," Cassie said. "You go that way —" She pointed to the south side of the porch— "and I'll go this way."

Hattie nodded and clomped off. Cassie headed left, peering into the first window. It was a small room, not much bigger than a closet without a stick of furniture. She moved on, rounding the corner and looking in the next window, this one showing the grand room that seemed to stretch on and on. She could make out the dark shadow of a couch and a few chairs. Maybe a coffee table. A staircase led up, but the faint moonlight filtering inside was the only light and she couldn't see any details...or evidence of any person.

She moved on, stopping where the porch ended, inter-secting with a different room in the house, this one with the faint glow of a lamp. She cupped her hands against the east facing window. It was a study with a spindly desk and single rail-backed chair. Mostly empty bookshelves lined one wall. A thin blanket pooled on the floor, and a book lay open on the desk, along with what looked like a box of stationary and several pens. So this was a room Perry Hubbard used, at least occasionally, but there was no sign of the woman herself.

Cassie and Hattie reconvened at the front door. "Anything?" Cassie asked.

"Not a creature was stirring, not even a mouse," Hattie said. Even in the low evening light, her lipstick practically glowed florescent. Her lungs had recovered, and she clomped down the porch steps, the unyielding wooden soles of her clogs like hammers against each piece of rotting wood. "Let's check the back."

Cassie followed, and they rounded the house on the left side, slipping through a break in the pampas grass. A half-rotted fence blocked their way, but Hattie felt along the wood until she found the clasp of a gate. She pulled the attached string and pushed the gate open. The gentle sound of the water lapping the shore was at odds with Cassie's heart pounding in her ears.

The house loomed up next to them, raised on pilings to keep intruding storm waters from encroaching into the structure. How much beach had there been in the 1800s when the sea captain built this place? More than now, she thought.

"Are there stairs?" she asked, trying to see through the growing darkness. Her eyes had adjusted, but the moonlight was dim, covered by whispering clouds.

"Over here." Hattie led the way toward the other side of the house, the deck jutting out overhead. Cassie's ankles twisted under the uneven sand, but Hattie forged ahead, her clogs like snowshoes in a powdery tundra, sinking, but not enough to upset her balance.

They'd just reached the opposite end of the deck when Hattie stopped short. "Lord a'mighty," she said in a hoarse whisper.

"What is it?" Cassie asked. The question blew away with

the breeze when she followed Hattie's gaze and saw the shape of a woman's body lying in the sand in front of them, the handle of an unopened black umbrella clutched in her hand.

There was no question about it. It was Perry Hubbard.

Chapter 9

"Murder begins where self-defense ends."
　　~Georg Buchner

assie sat in one teal Adirondack chair, the wooden slats pressing into her thighs, while Hattie sat in the other, cigarette dangling between her fingers. They both held mugs of the hot tea Cassie had insisted on making, if for no other reason to give herself something to do. The cloud cover had obliterated the moon's glow and the circling red and blue lights on the sheriff's car gave off an eerie glow.

Cassie stared at the house, the cool October air chilling her to the bone. She and Hattie had stood guard over Perry Hubbard's lifeless body until two county deputies arrived. One secured the scene while the other, a burly man with wiry eyebrows and long, bushy sideburns who looked like he could play Captain Ahab in a local theater production of Moby Dick, took their statements.

"*Perry Hubbard did not have a grandson*," Hattie announced.

"No grandson," the deputy repeated as he jotted something down in his little notepad, the circumference of his pudgy fingers five times that of the stubby pencil he held. He looked at Hattie. "And why is that important?"

"Because *your* people told Delilah Rose over at the garden center that Perry Hubbard's *grandson* called you to say they'd be out of town, but she doesn't *have* a grandson, so whoever made that call was *not* her grandson, which means it was someone else." She flung her arm out in the general direction of the back of the house, an unlit cigarette dangling from between her fingers. "Someone with nefarious intentions, by the looks of it."

The deputy nodded as he listened and tried to follow Hattie's long sentence. "Got it," he said, though Cassie wasn't sure he actually *did* get it.

"She was *murdered*," Hattie said, waggling her head. "There is no way she fell from her own deck."

The deputy stared at her. "And how are you so sure about that, Mrs. Pickle."

Hattie stuck her hands on her hips defiantly. "Ms. Pickle. I'm a women's libber."

The man's lips twitched. "Fine. *Ms.* Pickle, how do you know she didn't fall?"

The deputy had to be equal in age to her, but she wagged her finger at him as if she was scolding a child. "I've known that woman for years. You think she's suddenly gonna lean too far over the railing so her feet kick up behind her causing her to flip over? No. Way."

Cassie tried to imagine it happening the way Hattie described, but she couldn't. Hattie was right. It didn't make sense.

"So she was pushed, you're saying?" The deputy made another note on his pad.

"Obviously," Hattie said with a roll of her blue shadowed eyes. "Was there an intruder? A burglary?"

"Can't say, ma'am."

"Ms.," Hattie corrected.

"Right. Ms." He took Hattie's phone number then turned to Cassie. "Anything to add...Ms.?"

Cassie might have smiled at that under different circumstances, but with a dead woman on the beach, there wasn't any humor in this man's confusion over Miss, Ms., and Mrs. "How long has she been dead?" she asked.

The deputy frowned, his jowls heavy. "I can't tell you that."

Hattie scowled at him. "Can't, or won't, because the way I heard it from that funeral guy, Perry's been dead for a couple o' days."

The burly man sighed. "You could do my job, *Ms.* Pickle."

Hattie pushed her lips out defiantly and nodded. "Damn straight, I could."

"That *is* what the medical examiner said."

He escorted them from the front yard to the sidewalk, closing the iron gate behind them with a definitive click. They'd been officially removed from the crime scene.

Now, across the street, Cassie's thoughts strayed to the fluttering curtain she thought she'd seen earlier in the week. Was that *before* Mrs. Hubbard fell, or could it have been after? "What if someone's squatting in the house?" she mused.

Hattie turned her head, exhaling a cloud of smoke from the cigarette she'd finally lit. Cassie coughed and waved her hand.

Hattie took another drag before she smashed out the butt in the ashtray on the table between them, and exhaled —this time away from Cassie's face. "You mean living there?"

"If someone knew she lived alone...some drifter or something...it's possible."

"Anything's possible," Hattie said. She sipped her tea, leaving a pink lipstick stain on the mug. The woman had the longest lasting lipstick Cassie had ever seen.

They stayed on the porch a while longer. Cucumber sauntered up the porch steps, purring as she rubbed against Hattie's leg. Hattie patted her lap and Cucumber jumped up, settling herself into a little gray ball.

After another thirty minutes, Cassie's eyelids drooped. She stood. Glanced at the house across the street one more time. Blinked. Was that...?

"Did you see that?" she demanded.

"See what?" Hattie asked.

"The upstairs window. I think..." Her voice dropped to a whisper. "Someone's in there."

"Of course they are," Hattie said. "Those deputies have to check inside. Didn't you watch Hill Street Blues? *Let's be careful out there.* They can't leave any stone unturned."

Cassie shook her head. "No Hill Street Blues."

Hattie narrowed her eyes, the silver in her eyeshadow catching the glow of the porch light. "Cagney and Lacey, then."

Cassie and Lacy had talked about watching the show given Lacy's namesake in the title, but in the end, they'd opted for *Three's Company*, *The Love Boat*, and *The Facts of Life*. Ah, that George Clooney. She and Lacy had argued over who would marry him and have his children. "No Cagney and Lacey."

Hattie pshawed. "Watch any cop show and you'll see, they always check for possible suspects at the scene of the crime."

That made sense. Cassie relaxed. "I'm going in."

As Hattie waved the back of her hand at Cassie as she opened the screen door, the circling blue and red lights of the deputy' cars suddenly stopped. Cassie turned to see them driving away.

It was only later, as she lay tossing and turning in bed, that she realized there was no way someone could have gotten from the top floor of the house where she'd seen the shadow to the cars parked in front of the house quickly enough before the deputies drove off.

She was right. Someone was in that house.

Chapter 10

"Intuition is like reading a word without having to spell it out."
~Agatha Christie, *Murder at the Vicarage*

"*J* know I'm right," Cassie said. She cradled the pink phone between her shoulder and ear, absently wrapping the twisted cord around her hand, then unwinding it again.

The burly deputy from the night before, who she now knew was named Ron Bosworth, gave a heavy sigh. "We checked the house. Old coffee in the pot. A full gallon of milk in the refrigerator. Wet clothes in the washing machine. All this points to nobody living in the house for several days, which is consistent with the idea that Mrs. Hubbard has been dead for a few days. From the state of that house, the woman had a few screws loose. But there isn't a trace of evidence that someone else has been there with her."

Now Cassie gave an exasperated sigh. "I didn't say

someone was living there with her," she said, though she had thought it the night before. Squatters. "An intruder isn't going to make coffee or wash clothes."

Were they?

"Miss Lane, you did your duty reporting the body. You can forget about the whole thing now and go back to your flowers."

Cassie gave an aggravated scream as she slammed the handset back into place, the force making it ding. The gall! This man was the reason there were women's libbers in the first place. Go back to her flowers. As if.

Hattie shuffled into the kitchen, Cucumber in her arms, a hot pink terrycloth robe swinging from side to side revealing the polka dot nighty underneath. Her knobby knees looked even knobbier, her spindly legs spindlier with enormous lime green slippers on her feet. "What's goin' on, honey?"

Cassie told her.

She dropped Cucumber unceremoniously. The cat mewed in displeasure and sauntered off without a backwards glance.

Hattie didn't pay him any mind. She rubbed her hands together like they were two sticks and she was trying to start a fire. "Well, shoot, if that's how they're gonna play it, we'll just have to investigate ourselves. We'll be Cagney and Lacey."

Hattie changed clothes in seconds flat, her robe and slippers replaced with bellbottom jeans left over from the 70s and a long-sleeved black t-shirt. Cassie did a double take. She'd never seen Hattie in clothing so subdued.

"I don't want to draw attention," Hattie said, as if she'd read Cassie's mind.

"Right. No, of course." She didn't mention the bright

pink streaks in her hair or the florescent pink that permanently stained her lips.

They headed back across the street. Although the house was much less eerie in broad daylight, the knowledge that a woman had been found dead clouded Cassie's perception of the place. Compared to the bright magenta of Hattie's house, the old sea captain's house had an aura of sadness around it.

Hattie led the way through the iron gate, marched right up to the porch, and produced a key from her pant pocket.

Cassie stopped short at the top of the steps. "You have a key?"

Hattie shrugged. "I have a collection of keys. One for every house on Rum Runner's Lane, plus a few for Buccaneer. If anyone locks themselves out of their house, they come to me. I'm always here."

That was true. Hattie didn't seem to go anywhere or do anything. She lived in the house she'd grown up in. She owned it, free and clear. She collected rent from Cassie, sure, but she must have other money to live off of because she didn't have a job. In fact, Cassie had no idea what Hattie did all day while she was off working at the garden center. When she'd asked her once, Hattie had given a closed-lip smile and shrugged. "This 'n that."

"Why didn't you use it the other night?"

"We were in a hurry," Hattie said. "I forgot."

Cassie remembered Hattie muttering something about a key under her breath when they'd gotten to the door. Now that made sense.

She held the screen door while Hattie inserted a key painted with pink nail polish into the lock and turned it. She pushed the door in, then quietly closed it again once they were both inside. She spun around and held a finger to her fuchsia lips. Cassie nodded, following Hattie as they tiptoed forward.

Hattie stopped short and flung out one arm. The clunking of her wooden-soled clogs was muffled against the linoleum floor, but still loud enough to sound like an alarm in the silence.

"Whoops!" she said in a too-loud whisper, and she slipped out of them. While her clothes were subdued, her socks were not. Bright pink, green, blue, and yellow stripes ran like ladder rungs up the top of her feet, disappearing under the wide legs of her pants.

She tried again, holding a finger to her lips, and tiptoeing across the room while Cassie waited, her breath frozen in her lungs.

Hattie reached the center of the room. She stopped, put a palm to her chest, then pointed upstairs. Cassie nodded. "Be careful," she mouthed before putting her own hand to her chest and pointing toward the back of the house and what she thought was probably the kitchen.

They separated. Hattie's back hunched and she bent her legs and arms, creeping across the room like a cat burglar from a B movie.

Cassie laughed to herself as she did the same thing, her footsteps silent as she crossed the massive room, giving the couch, chairs, and table a cursory glance. Everything looked the same as it had when she'd peered in through the window the evening before.

One of her sneakers suddenly squeaked. She froze. Held her breath. Maybe she was being paranoid. The shadow she thought she'd seen had probably been her imagination.

She released her breath and hurried on, stopping once she made it into the kitchen. A few dishes sat in the sink, left over from Perry Hubbard's last meal. The square tiles on the countertops had dark grout. A small white bag had been shoved into a corner of the counter. The delivery from the other day, most likely.

The sink was dark. Cassie had a fleeting thought that the place could stand a remodel. A beach house should have a beach feeling. Light and airy, not dark and weighted down with earth tones.

She let the thought go and opened the refrigerator. A glow beamed out like a lighthouse beacon, but in the broad daylight, it didn't matter. A putrid smell wafted out. Cassie scrunched her nose and sniffed. That was silly, though. She wasn't about to toss anything out, so it didn't matter what had turned rotten since Perry Hubbard had died.

The container of milk was there, just like the deputy had said. A jar of applesauce. A soggy head of lettuce. She closed the door and moved on. Cassie walked past the kitchen table and what she now realized was a double-sided fireplace. She caught her breath as she glanced out the plate glass windows at the uninterrupted view of Roanoke Sound and the barrier island beyond.

It was a million-dollar view.

She kept going, glancing in the laundry room at the washer and dryer, a pile of clothes in the basket. A slow drip, drip, drip came from the leaky faucet of the utility sink. The floor above her creaked and her eyes shot to the ceiling. Even under the careful prowling of the Pink Panther, the floors of an old house were likely to groan. Cassie held her breath, but the sound didn't repeat. She went back the way she'd come and into the small room just off the left side of the kitchen. It was sparse. A thin yellow blanket was draped over the back of the desk chair. Only a few books and knick-knacks sat on the built-in shelves. She backed out and went to the kitchen for one last look at the Sound. For a moment, her gaze stopped on the deck and the spot Mrs. Hubbard had probably stood. Hattie's description of Mrs. Hubbard falling came back to her mind. It *couldn't* have happened accidentally, but that meant someone had pushed her.

Who would have done that, and why?

Chapter 11

"Hope is necessary in every condition."
~*Samuel Johnson*

assie stared at Hattie. "What do you mean?"

The older woman fumbled with a cigarette, dropping it after she slid it from the pouch she carried them in. "Just what I said. It's a construction zone."

They'd crossed the street in a hurry, with Hattie dragging Cassie by her sweater sleeve, stopping only once they were back in Hattie's little courtyard. "The floors are torn up. There's holes in the walls. It's demolished."

"Was she remodeling?" Cassie asked, but she knew immediately that *that* didn't make sense. There'd been no work trucks around. No dumpster in the yard or on the street. If she was remodeling, there would have been the bustle of people in and out of the house, taking out debris and bringing in new materials.

There also would have been noise. Hammering and sawing.

"Cassandra Lane, you are not hearin' me," Hattie said, her voice bordering on hysterical. "Someone is tearin' that house apart, bit by bit."

The deputy's comment about Mrs. Hubbard's mental stability came back to her. *From the state of the house, she had a few screws loose*, he'd said.

Cassie pictured the dead woman's figure on the sand behind the house. The umbrella clutched in her arthritic hands. Gripping hammers and crowbars and whatever else was needed to pry up floorboards and pound through walls would have been too much for the elderly woman. She asked Hattie about it anyway. "Could Mrs. Hubbard have been the one tearing it up?"

Hattie scoffed, putting a definitive Kabash to Cassie's question. "Not in ten million years," she said before sucking in a ragged breath and breaking into a coughing frenzy. It was hoarse and rattled her bones. She bent at the waist, hands on her thighs.

Which meant someone else had been doing the dirty work either *for* or *in spite of* Mrs. Hubbard.

While it was one hundred percent possible that Mrs. Hubbard had hired someone to tear up her house—either to remodel or to look for something—Cassie knew that wasn't what had happened. The woman owned the house, so there was no reason to hide the fact that she had people working on it.

Several realizations hit her all at once, the thoughts chasing around her brain like a cat after a mouse. The day she and Hattie had found Perry Hubbard's body, the deputy had said there was almost a full gallon of milk in the fridge.

When she'd looked, it had been closer to empty.

He'd said there were wet clothes in the washing machine, but when Cassie looked in the laundry room, the lid to the machine had been up, a small pile of what looked like clean clothes piled on top of the dryer.

She thought about the grocery and pharmacy deliveries. If Mrs. Hubbard had already been dead...

She came back to her theory about squatters. Had it actually been Mrs. Hubbard who'd opened the door, or had it been someone else? Could the murderer have been in the house all along?

Something else surfaced in her mind. The line from the book she'd bought at The Open Door:

"Were Mahtob and I prisoners? Hostages? Captives of this venomous stranger who had once been a loving husband and father?"

WHAT IF IT hadn't been about Faith Dresher at all?

Cassie's eyelids pricked. What if it was Mrs. Hubbard who'd been hostage in her own house?

She couldn't stop the tears from falling. This. This was why she hated her divination. If she had interpreted the book magic differently, maybe Mrs. Hubbard would still be alive.

A vice clamped around her heart. Oh no, no, no.

Chapter 12

"One day you will do things for me that you hate. That is what it means to be family."

~Jonathan Safran Foer, *Everything Is Illuminated*

*C*assie lay on her back, her legs hanging over the side, feeling small and wishing more than anything that she'd never given into the book magic temptation. If only she'd never gone into The Open Door and seen that stupid book. Because now Perry Hubbard was dead and maybe she could have stopped it.

Before she'd collapsed onto her bed, she'd stretched the long, twisty cord from the phone's base on her bedside table, dialed, and clutched the handset to her ear. Her heart had sputtered when she'd heard Aunt Rose's familiar voice, but the feeling passed quickly. Her aunt was not making her feel one iota better.

"Cassandra, depth of understanding comes with practice," her aunt said. "And you stopped practicing."

Cassie cringed. Aunt Rose only called her Cassandra when she was disappointed. Cassie wanted to yell, "*I never asked for this!*" Instead she sighed and said, "I'm done."

Aunt Rose responded with an exasperated, "You've said that before, but you always come back to it. You can't hide from who you are. You'll find peace when you embrace it."

The words seemed to hang above her, suspended from the popcorn ceiling by gossamer threads. Cassie swatted them away. She didn't want annoying platitudes. She wanted to stop the Lane curse.

No, she *needed* to stop it.

She wanted to go back in time and interpret the message from that book correctly so Perry Hubbard would still be alive.

And now she wanted to find out what the secrets were on Rum Runner's Lane. To find out who did this to the old woman.

But could she do that without resorting to bibliomancy.

"Faith Dresher disappeared," Cassie said to her aunt. "She disappeared, so of course I interpreted those lines from that stupid book to be about *that*."

"*That* was an unfortunate distraction."

That was one way to put it. Aunt Rose wasn't the placating type. Cassie wanted her to say it wasn't her fault. Instead, she said, "Think about your gift in the same way as having the ability to speak a foreign language. You get rusty if you don't use it. You forget the vocabulary. You don't understand it as well. But when you practice, you get better. You gain *fluency*."

"It's my curse, not my gift," Cassie said, correcting her aunt, because bibliomancy was hardly a gift when all it did was alert her to calamities she was unable to stop, or to tragedies yet to be that—that she *also* could not stop.

"You girls," Aunt Rose said, the two words heavy with her irritation. "I did my best, you know."

Cassie sat up, rearranging herself into a cross-legged position in the center of her bed. "You did great considering what you had to work with," she said, the tables suddenly turned so that she was the one reassuring her aunt instead of the other way around. "How's Lacy?"

"She's right here," Aunt Rose said, and before Cassie could stop her, she heard the clatter of the phone as it dropped to a table.

A few seconds later, Lacy's flat voice said, "Nice of you to call."

"Communication is a two-way street, Lace," she shot back, the words out before she could stop them. In five words, her sister could get her hackles up.

"That's rich. *You're* the one who left. *You* should be the one who calls."

Cassie didn't bother to point out her sister's flawed logic. She didn't want to fight with Lacy. She wanted to hear the lightness and excitement her sister used to exude when they were younger. "I'll call more often," Cassie promised.

"Whatever."

Cassie's jaw tightened. She had to remember that Lacy was just seventeen. She was still in the thick of her terrible teens, and Cassie was at the center of her sister's angst because of whatever betrayal Lacy had seen.

Cassie forced another minute of strained conversation, but her sister wasn't interested. Finally, they hung up, and Cassie felt worse than she had before the phone call. She lay in bed, replaying the conversations with her aunt and her sister. The one thing she kept coming back to was Aunt Rose saying that Faith Dresher's disappearance a distraction.

That implied that the book magic had nothing to do with her, but was that true?

Chapter 13

"Yeah, as long as we know we're trapped, we still have a chance to escape."
~Sara Grant, Neva

Cassie held the hose out in front of her to avoid the drips from the leaking nozzle. If she held it too close, the water trickled down her arm and soaked her entire front. Delilah, she'd realized, did not have time for things like replacing a worn out washer. Cassie would stop at the hardware store sometime soon to take care of it herself.

The garden center was busy for a Wednesday afternoon. Men and women milled around, some in shorts, still hanging onto the hope of an October heatwave. A man in a ballcap looked intently at the impatiens. Another wearing a down vest with a pair of khaki shorts examined a sad little lemon tree leftover from spring. A woman pushing a baby stroller walked up the aisle, but instead of looking at the flats of flowers, her gaze was pinned on Cassie.

"How old is your baby?" Cassie asked, releasing the nozzle lever and holding the hose away from her body to avoid the dribbling spray.

"Four months." No smile. No animation at all, in fact. The woman looked like she wanted to bolt, but she stayed put.

Cassie bent to get a closer look, letting her fingertips flutter over the yellow blanket draped over the sleeping infant. The baby's light eyebrows lifted and her eyelids stretched. Her tiny hands fisted and she wriggled in the pram, readjusting herself before everything relaxed again. A small pang of longing flitted through Cassie. Would she be a good mother? The question flitted in and out of her mind before she could grab hold of it. She straightened up, tamping down the ache. "She's so precious."

The woman's face softened. She leaned over and tucked the blanket around the baby's shape. "She is."

"What's her name?"

"Audrey," the woman said.

Cassie smiled. Somehow the baby looked like an Audrey, although she didn't know how that was possible. She held up one finger to tell the woman *wait one sec*, then hurried to the end of the aisle to turn off the spigot. She dropped the hose, turning to give the woman her full attention. "What can I help you with?"

The woman hesitated and for a second it looked like she'd changed her mind. Like she was going to turn around after all, but she cleared her throat and lifted her chin. "I... um...I think I won something? A garden makeover?"

Cassie's heart expanded inside her ribcage. "Oh my gosh, yes! Are you—?"

The woman nodded. "Faith."

Cassie clasped her hands together. "Faith! Right! It's great to meet you!"

"I don't know how I won—"

Cassie interrupted her with a wave of her hand. "All that matters is that you *did* win."

Something over Cassie's shoulder caught Faith's eye. Her eyes glazed and she nodded. Some*one*, Cassie realized.

She squeezed her hands around the handle of the stroller. Nerves. "Do I, um, have to buy anything?"

Cassie shook her head. "Not at all. It's completely free." At least to Faith it would be. Cassie would have to buy the plants with her own money and work on the yard during her free time, but that was okay with her if it helped her help Faith. And looking at the woman's timid expression, Cassie knew Faith needed help. A lot of help.

"We gotta go."

A man's voice came from right behind Cassie, the words practically echoing in her ear. She jumped and started to turn, but the baby's sudden cry made her stop. Faith rocked the stroller back and forth until Audrey settled back into her slumber. "But she said—"

"Now!" The man's voice was a whisper yell and Faith jerked and started to turn the stroller around.

"You can go this way," Cassie said. She moved out of the way so Faith could pass her by, sneaking a glance at the man she assumed was Mr. Dresher. He was already heading into the garden shop, apparently confident in the fact that his wife would follow right behind him.

"Faith," Cassie said quietly. "If there's anything I can do—"

Mr. Dresher's hard voice cut her off from halfway across the nursery. "Let's. Go."

Faith's entire body seemed to fold in on itself. She didn't look at Cassie again, just pushed the stroller past her. Cassie watched as she walked away. Before Faith got to the garden shop's door, she put her hand behind her back, palm out.

Cassie blinked. Something was written there. She hurried after her. "Faith?"

Faith slid her hand further up her back, and that's when Cassie saw it. Written in black Sharpie was a number.

"Wait!" Cassie yelled, but Faith disappeared into the shop behind her husband. A second later, she was in the parking lot with Mr. Dresher's hand clamped firmly around Faith's wrist. He walked fast, dragging his wife alongside, the stroller rocking precariously as Faith tried to steady it. Cassie watched helplessly as they got to the end of the parking lot. He took the baby from the stroller and practically thrust her at Faith. He collapsed the stroller and threw it into the back of the car while Faith put the baby into the back seat, taking enough time to make Cassie think she'd secured Audrey into a car seat.

Something niggled in her brain. The man? The car? Cassie tried to pin it down, but wherever it was, it was just out of reach. Mr. Dresher slammed the tailgate closed. Just before he got into the driver's side of the car, he turned so, finally, Cassie could see his face and recognition hit.

Mr. Dresher had been the man with the Walkman delivering groceries to Perry Hubbard from Sadler's.

Chapter 14

"We must not allow other people's limited perceptions to define us."
   ~Virginia Satir

Cassie's thoughts collided in her head. Carl Dresher *knew* Perry Hubbard through grocery deliveries, but so what? Just because he was a horrible husband didn't mean he had anything to do with what happened to Perry Hubbard. Coincidences happened all the time.

Why had Mr. Dresher bothered to bring his wife to the garden center? The only logical answer was that he was trying to placate Faith. After all, she'd run away, but come back. Maybe the garden makeover was a carrot. A carrot he'd summarily yanked at the last second. To keep Faith off guard? Under his thumb? He'd clearly shown her who was in charge—as if she needed any reminding.

That led her back to why Faith had run in the first place,

but *The Unbearable Lightness of Being* had given her the answer before she'd even known what the question was.

> *"A person who longs to leave the place where he lives is an unhappy person."*

HER THOUGHTS HAD SPUN around in a split second, and now she raced to the garden shop's checkout counter.

Faith had been unhappy enough to leave. It didn't take book magic to know why she'd come back. Cassie pictured the book jacket of *Not Without My Daughter*. Those words—the title—had turned darker under Cassie's gaze. *That* was the message—or at least one of the messages—that book was telling her. Faith couldn't leave her husband without taking Audrey with her. She'd tried, but she'd come back, and now she was stuck.

Delilah watched her dial 911, raising her brows at her as she spoke into the receiver, telling the man on the other end of the line that Faith Dresher's life was in danger. "She had 911 written on her hand," Cassie said for the second time, trying not to shout as she explained what she'd seen.

"Do you have a license plate number?" he asked.

"No, but it's a dark green Range Rover and it belongs to Mr. Carl Dresher. They live on Magpie Lane."

"I can send a car to check on the woman, but—"

"Fine, great, thank you," Cassie said before slamming the phone back into its cradle. She knew what the man had been about to say. But they couldn't do anything if there was no evidence of abuse and if Faith didn't say anything.

Cassie grabbed her purse from the shelf under the counter, digging her truck keys from it. "I have to—"

"Go!" Delilah waved one hand toward the door. "Go now."

A scant minute later, Cassie sped away, heading for Magpie Lane.

Chapter 15

"Blessed are you who endure life trails."
   ~Lailah Gifty Akita

*E*ither the police had already come and gone, or Cassie beat them to the Dresher's house. Either way, the army green Range Rover wasn't there. She slammed to a stop in front of the house anyway, racing to the front door and pounding on it. "Faith! Are you in there? Faith!"

No answer.

She ran to the backyard, barreling through the chain link gate and checking the backdoor. Locked. She peered through the windows at the kitchen. No sign of life.

Her heart beat erratically in her chest. She had to find Faith. The woman had written 911 on her hand. It was a call for help, and Cassie had to answer that call, but she didn't know what to do. Where to go.

Back in the front yard, she looked up and down the

street as if she expected the Dresher's car to appear. Of course, it didn't. She dug her fingers through her hair, pressing her fingernails against her scalp as she turned in a circle, feeling helpless.

Finally, she got back in her truck and headed to Hattie's house. From there, she could call the sheriff's department again. She backtracked, passing the garden center, driving toward town, turning onto Buccaneer Lane and slowing to what felt like a painful crawl as she dropped down to the twenty mile per hour residential speed limit. Her knuckles turned white as she fisted her hands on the steering wheel, elbows locked. Where had they gone?

She made a hard left, turning onto Rum Runner's Lane. No one was behind her, but out of habit, she flicked on her turn signal before doing a three-point turn and directing her truck south so she could park on Hattie's side of the street.

Out of habit, she looked at Mrs. Hubbard's house. For so long she'd wanted to see inside the beautiful old house, but when she finally had, it had been under an aura of death. Be careful what you wish for.

The bright, colorful flowers she'd planted were now a physical juxtaposition to the cluster of dark clouds hovering over the house. She blinked. Looked away. Let her gaze drift down the street. And then she started. There, parked along the street on the other side just before Perry Hubbard's house, was Carl Dresher's Range Rover.

How had she missed it?

Why was it here?

Once again, she thought about the lines from *Not Without My Daughter*. Were they hostages? Captives?

Her blood ran cold and goosebumps flared on the

surface of her skin as the truth hit. The message from that book was just as much about Perry Hubbard as it was about Faith Dresher. Mrs. Hubbard had been a hostage. Faith Dresher still was.

Cassie hadn't seen Perry Hubbard for several days before she and Hattie discovered the old woman's body. Could Mrs. Hubbard have been a prisoner in her own house, held captive by Carl Dresher? What if she'd managed to escape, only to get pushed over the back railing?

Cassie knew what she had to do. She careened through the house, dropping her purse on one of the purple chairs, and hollered for Hattie.

There was no answer, so Cassie went straight to the drawer in the kitchen where Hattie had dropped the key to Perry Hubbard's house after they'd come back that night. When Hattie had said she had keys to all her neighbor's houses, she wasn't kidding. The drawer swam with them. Cassie ran her hands over them, spreading them out.

There it was. The key with the pink nail polish.

She grabbed it, situating it in her hand so the hard metal poked out from between two fingers. It wasn't much of a weapon, but at least it was something.

Next, she snatched up the receiver of the wall-mounted kitchen phone, and dialed 911, nervously tapping her foot and twisting the phone's cord around her hand. A woman said, "911, what is your emergency?"

She skipped the story about visiting the Dresher's house to find it empty, thankful the same man hadn't answered, and said the only thing she could think of that would elicit a response.

"There's an intruder!"

"Ma'am. Calm down ma'am."

"There's an intruder!" The house numbers on Perry

Hubbard's home flashed in her mind and she rattled them off. "2930 Rum Runner's Lane. Please hurry!"

The woman on the phone started to say something, but Cassie dropped the receiver. It hit the linoleum with a dull thud.

Seconds later, she was across the street and plowing up the front walkway, hoping Carl wasn't inside peering down at her through one of the windows.

Her heart ratcheted up, though, when she remembered the fluttering curtain the night they'd found Mrs. Hubbard. Had he been in the house when they'd searched it? If so, where had he hidden?

She quickly unlocked the front door and slipped inside. It was dark and dreary, the windows letting in only a small bit of light from the cloud-covered sky. She paused long enough to let her eyes adjust before creeping forward. She took an immediate left, turning to peek into the small study she'd seen through the window the first time she and Hattie had come to the house. It was still empty.

She moved through the main room, thanking the stars above that her sneakers were silent against the linoleum floor. Was there hardwood underneath? she wondered. The question dissolving the moment it registered in her brain.

She peered in the kitchen. Everything looked the same as it had the last time. After making sure the laundry room was empty, she went to the study. It was the last downstairs room to check. Next, she'd go upstairs, all the way to the widow's walk if she needed to.

As she stopped in the doorway of the study, she had a flash of her first visit to this room. A blanket had lain over the back of the desk chair. A yellow baby's blanket she now realized—just like the one in Audrey's baby stroller. One and the same? Had Faith and Audrey had been in this room?

She stepped in, holding her breath as she jerked the door toward her, half expecting someone to jump out from behind it.

She heaved a sigh of relief. Nothing.

She didn't dare flip on the light switch. She didn't want to alert Carl to her presence, if he was here in the house somewhere. Her breath, so loud in her ears, seemed like a foghorn cutting through the silence. There was no other place to hide in the room. She peered under the desk. Empty. She looked behind the door again, like she might have missed something the first time. Still no one there.

Anxiety infused frustration bubbled up inside her. They'd been here—the blanket was proof of that—but they weren't here now. She started to turn, stopping suddenly when she heard something.

She held her breath as she listened.

Had it come from upstairs somewhere, carried through the ceiling? Somebody crying?

She willed her heartbeat to stop its relentless pounding as she cocked her head, listening for it again.

There it was! It was the frantic, breath gasping sound of a baby crying.

Audrey.

A single word from the Mahmoudi book echoed in her head. *Hostage. Hostage. Hostage.*

Throwing away all caution, she ran from the room, taking the stairs to the second floor two at a time, jigging and jagging between the torn-up floorboards. She went through each room, listening for the baby and feeling like she was playing a game of Hot and Cold.

As she moved toward the south side of the house, the crying grew fainter.

As she moved to the north end, it became more audible, but still muffled.

In one of the back bedrooms, where the sound was loudest, she pressed her ear to the wall. It was coming from behind it, she was sure of it.

Where was the door? She searched, pressing her ear to the wall, listening, running her palms across it, feeling for some sort of hidden access. She looked in the closet, thinking there might be an attic access.

Nothing.

She wanted to call out to Faith, but she kept quiet. She'd already revealed herself by running through the house. If, on the off chance that it was Carl with Audrey and he hadn't heard her footsteps pounding against the stairs as she'd ascended, she didn't want to give herself away now.

Cassie went back to the downstairs study. She didn't think there could be access from there, but she had nowhere else to look. Every room upstairs had been a dead end.

She stopped just inside the doorway to listen again, her breath catching in her throat when she heard footsteps above her. Faith—or possibly Carl—but most likely Faith was walking around, probably bouncing a bundled up little Audrey in her arms, trying to get her to settle down.

The low murmur of a woman's voice drifted through the ceiling. There was no hint of a man's voice. No Carl berating his wife to keep the baby quiet. That was a good sign.

With no evidence of an entry, Cassie called out in as loud a voice as she dared, "Faith? It's Cassie. I'm here, Faith."

The murmurs stopped, but Audrey's crying continued.

"Faith, where are you?"

There was no response for a moment, then came the

sound a thud and Faith's voice, louder, as if she'd fallen to the ground and was speaking to her through a hole in the floor. "There as hid—doo—"

The baby's wails—because that's what they were now, wails—overpowered Faith's voice.

"Say it again," Cassie told her.

Cassie thought she heard Faith shushing Audrey, then her voice came again. "Hidden...door."

A hidden door! Just like in an old Vincent Price movie. Cassie swung her head around, scanning the room. "Where," she asked, her head tilted back, her words directed toward the ceiling. She redirected her focus toward the bookshelves along the back wall of the room at what sounded like footsteps descending a staircase.

A hidden door leading to a staircase? She searched the shelves, shoving the few books housed there out of the way. "Where? Where's the door?"

The footsteps stopped, replaced by Audrey's whimpering. She'd stopped crying, as if she knew her wails were preventing her mother from communicating with Cassie. Then pounding came. "I'm here," Faith called, her voice still muffled, but closer than it had been a moment before.

Cassie searched, running her hands over the shelves and along the back.

Nothing.

Faith said something, but Audrey had started up again, Faith's words caught up between the cries. Cassie tried again, this time running her hands up and down the vertical pieces of wood separating each section of shelving. She gasped. There was a gap! Paper thin, but it was there. She felt around for a lever. A handle. Anything that would allow a secret door to open.

When she didn't find anything, she went to the other

side of that shelving section, feeling along the vertical line of wood. There it was. Another gap between the wood.

She scanned from the ceiling to the ground, curled her fingers around the edge of the vertical trim, feeling underneath it. Searching. Searching. And then her fingers touched something. A sliding lock, MacGyvered so the barrel bolt disappeared into the wood itself. She pried at it, finally pulling it free.

"Push it open!" Cassie called.

She heard the force of what she thought was Faith throwing her body against the inside of the door. She stepped out of the way as it swung open.

Cassie rushed forward to pull Faith and Audrey from their captivity, stopping short as Faith looked over Cassie's shoulder, her expression morphing from elated to horrified.

At the same moment, Cassie heard the floor creak behind her. She darted to her left as a hand came down, skimming off her shoulder, unable to make purchase. Carl stumbled, falling to the ground. The crack of his Walkman hitting the floor and skittering away was followed by the hard thud of his shoulder.

The tinny sound of music wafted from his foam earphones. No wonder he hadn't heard her.

From her peripheral vision, Cassie saw Faith frozen in the threshold of the hidden doorway. Cassie scurried around Carl to grab Faith's arm. She yanked her forward, praying Faith would be able to hold onto the baby.

Carl was up on his feet again, grunting. He stood now with his back to the secret doorway, staring them down. Cassie shoved Faith and Audrey behind her, Audrey's ear-piercing wails frantic now. Cassie bent her knees and readied herself like she remembered David Carradine doing in old reruns of Kung Fu. She was no match for Carl—she knew that—but she was determined.

Behind her, Faith sobbed. "Carl. It's okay. I'll go back in."

Carl let his eyes leave Cassie for a split second to look at his wife. "Shut her up," he growled, his words nearly drowned out by Audrey's cries.

That moment was the only opportunity Cassie needed. She lunged forward, shoving Carl's chest with every ounce of strength she had. The force caught Carl by surprise. He lurched backward, his feet tangling. He went down with a sickening thud, the back of his head hitting the first step of the staircase.

Faith gasped, but she reacted quicker than Cassie did. She put the distraught Audrey on the ground, pulling the corner of the yellow blanket up under the baby's head. In a flash Faith was at Carl's feet. For a moment, Cassie thought she was going to go to him, to check if he was alright.

But as Carl stirred, a low groan escaping his lips, Faith flew into action. She grabbed hold of Carl's boots, shoving them into the hidden space. "Close it!"

Her voice was frantic. Cassie leapt to the open door. Carl twisted his body, kicking his feet as he tried to dislodge Faith's hands and flip himself over to his hands and knees. Cassie's heart rocketed to her throat, fear of shutting Faith up into the room with Carl spreading through her like an oil spill. But she shoved the door closed, trusting Faith. At the last second, Faith released Carl's feet and jumped clear of the threshold. She whipped around, helping Cassie push the door all the way closed, then flipped, pressing her back against the shelves, holding it closed while Cassie snatched up the barrel lock and plowed it back into place.

They both bent over, hands on knees. Cassie tried to calm her ratcheting breath. On the floor, Audrey's cries had died down to a low simper—as if she knew she was finally safe.

"He can't hurt you anymore," Cassie said to Faith.

Tears streamed down Faith's cheeks. She fell to her knees at Audrey's side. "Daddy can't hurt us anymore," she repeated.

Chapter 16

"Actions are the seed of fate."
~Harry S Truman

*H*attie picked up a hot pink pouch, opened the clasp, and withdrew a cigarette, slipping it between her lips. She slipped a Bic lighter from the front pocket. Cupping one hand around it, she flicked it to life and sucked in. The end of the cigarette hissed as the flame caught. She took one deep inhalation before taking it from her mouth and expelling the smoke.

Cassie frowned. If it was the last thing she did, she was going to get Hattie to quit smoking.

Hattie spoke in-between puffs on her cigarette. "I heard from Madelyn Rochester who heard from Marie Bullworth who heard it from Lindy Swartz whose husband works for the county DA that Carl Dresher's been charged with kidnapping and unlawful restraint."

They sat on the porch in the Adirondack chairs. Cassie

crossed one side of her sweater over the other against the crisp October air. She and Hattie looked across the street at Perry Hubbard's house. The dark clouds had lifted, the sky above so blue Cassie thought it could absorb any darkness.

"Faith said Carl was looking for the sea captain's buried treasure. He was convinced it was hidden in the house somewhere."

Hattie snorted. "People believe what they want to believe. That man's not the first one to search for treasure in that house. I told you, there's all kinds of secrets on this island."

Mrs. Hubbard's house was at least a hundred and fifty years old. Maybe more. If that old sea captain had buried something, surely it would have been found by now. If it hadn't, the odds were good he never had a treasure in the first place. "Do you think it ever existed?" Cassie asked her.

"Could be," Hattie said with a shrug.

That was a non-answer if there ever was one. "Did you know about the hidden room?"

Hattie took a drag of her cigarette, releasing the smoke before she answered. "Perry mentioned it once or twice. Can't say as I'm surprised. It's just another secret on Rum Runner's Lane."

Chapter 17

"When everything goes to hell, the people who stand by you without flinching -- they are your family."
~Jim Butcher

The package came in the mail exactly one month to the day after Cassie had rescued Faith and Audrey Dresher. Cassie had been true to her word, devoting her spare time to redoing Faith's yard. Now that Carl was locked away for the murder of Perry Hubbard and the kidnapping of his own wife and child, Faith was free. She'd become another friend in Cassie's growing community.

But this package was from her family. Her heart climbed to her throat as she read the return address.

Laurel Point, Oregon.

She tore off the brown paper and pulled apart the flaps of the cardboard box. A small lavender envelope sat on top of the paper that wrapped whatever was inside. Cassie lifted the flap, pulling out a card from Aunt Rose's custom stationary—the Cape Misery lighthouse, in all its glory, a sign above the door that said Books By Bequest.

My dear Cassandra,

The enclosed necklace belonged to your mother, and your grandmother Emily, and great-great grandmother Siobhan before that. Your mother intended you to have it when you turned twenty. I've been its keeper, but now I am passing it to you. With it, may you hold Annabel close to your heart.

With love,
Aunt Rose

P.S. The book is from your sister

CASSIE SET the card down and gingerly peeled back the tissue paper inside the box. She took out the small bundle first, carefully opening the small drawstring velvet bag. She pulled out the necklace, holding it by its chain. Cassie knew it was white gold—not silver—the precious metal her mother, and all the Lane women, had preferred according to Aunt Rose. On one side was a Fleur de Lis, embossed into the gold. On the back were two trees, and something else she couldn't quite make out.

The pendant was rustic and beautiful. Exactly what Cassie would have picked for herself, made all the more special because it had come from Annabel.

She unclasped the chain, strung it around her neck, and refastened it. The pendant was cool against her skin, but instantly warmed, the weight of it grounding. For a moment, she felt as if she were back at the hilltop cemetery at Cape Misery where she'd always felt closest to her parents.

She blinked away the tears that threatened, pulling the other gift from the box. She unwrapped the tissue and held the book in her hands. *The Unbearable Lightness of Being*.

It didn't frighten her like books usually did. She hadn't been able to save Perry Hubbard, but she'd saved Faith Dresher from her husband—all thanks to her bibliomancy. Maybe she could find a middle ground.

She opened the front cover to reveal a note.

Cass,

I realized something the other day. I drove you away. That's the betrayal I saw. I did it to myself! Stupid, stupid, stupid. I've been wishing you'd come back, but this book told me something. You're meant to stay where you are. Your future is there.

I'll always love you.
Lacy

P.S. I'm pregnant!

CASSIE'S SMILE FADED. Pregnant. That wasn't possible. Well, it was possible, but they'd made a deal. A pact. The Lane curse meant that the women in the family would ultimately be taken during childbirth. Their mother had survived Cassie's birth, but not Lacy's. The Lane curse had been fulfilled.

Her head suddenly felt heavy, her skin pricking from the inside out. Lacy could not be pregnant.

Except Cassie knew that she was.

A movement at the window caught her eye. She glanced up and started. A black crow sat on the sill outside, its glassy eyes trained on her. Cassie's skin turned cold. She'd always believed the crow was not a harbinger of darkness and death, but of new beginnings.

Not this one. Her fingers tightened on the book, that old feeling returning. It suddenly felt like a hot potato she wanted to fling away.

Instead, she drew in a breath and flipped through the pages, watching the blur of words. And then she stopped. This book had told Lacy so much. It had rectified a wrong, and led Lacy to forgiveness. Could it alleviate Cassie's concern for her sister?

She cracked the book open, then rested it on its spine. She closed her eyes and murmured the first question that came to mind. "Will Lacy be okay?"

The book fell open. Cassie opened her eyes. A passage darkened, the words undulating as they lifted off the page, growing larger as if she were viewing them through a magnifying glass. She held her breath as she read.

"The heaviest of burdens crushes us, we sink beneath it, it pins us to the ground. But in love poetry of every age, the woman longs to be weighed down by the man's body. The heaviest of burdens is therefore simultaneously an image of life's most intense fulfillment. The heavier the burden, the closer our lives come to the earth, the more real and truthful they become. Conversely, the absolute absence of burden causes man to be lighter than air, to soar into heights, take leave of the earth and his earthly being, and become only half real, his movements as

free as they are insignificant. What then shall we choose?
Weight or lightness?"

CASSIE LET OUT A SHAKY BREATH. One line was darker than
the rest, riffling in the air, drawing attention to itself.

"...the absolute absence of burden causes man to be lighter than
air, to soar into heights, take leave of the earth and his earthly
being..."

CASSIE'S EYES pooled with tears as she interpreted the line.
Lacy felt freed from the burden of her anger toward Cassie.
She was making plans to have the baby she always wanted,
but felt she never could. She was letting go of her burdens,
and with the lightness that followed, she'd be taken from
this world.

She threw the book across the room. And Cassie, even
knowing her sister's fate, was helpless to stop it.

The End

Dear Reader,

I know you have many choices when it comes to books.
I'm thrilled you selected The Secret on Rum Runner's
Lane, the first Book Magic Mini Mystery. Readers often

decide what to read based on reviews. If you would, please take a moment to share your thoughts about this book. Thank you, and happy reading!

Leave a review on Amazon and Goodreads.

Start reading Murder in Devil's Cove, a Book Magic Mystery #1

Turn the page to read an excerpt from Murder in Devil's Cove, the first Book Magic Mystery.

"Some places speak distinctly. Certain dark gardens cry aloud for a murder; certain old houses demand to be haunted; certain coasts are set apart for shipwreck."
~Robert Louis Stevenson

Cassandra Lane Hawthorne stood on the main fishing pier in Devil's Cove staring out at the harbor, grasping the pendant she wore around her neck. The breeze blew across the Sound, whipping her hair into her face. The same feeling of foreboding she'd had since the day she'd met her husband filled her. Her insides were a dry sponge slowly expanding with water. "You're not going to take him," she said. Her voice was carried away on the breath of wind. She spoke again, louder this time. "You won't take him!"

"Take who, Mama?" Cassie's six-year-old daughter, Pippin, tugged at the fabric of Cassie's dress.

"Nobody." She took Pippin's hand and squeezed. "It's cold. Come on, let's go home."

They walked along the wooden slats of the pier, Cassie's white canvas sneakers silent next to the *slap slap slap* of

Pippin's sandals. The irony of her daughter's name wasn't lost on Cassie. Leo was a Tolkien fanatic. He and a group of friends had called themselves The Fellowship all through college. And when it came time to name their children, he'd longed for names from Tolkien's classics. Their son, born seventy-three seconds before Pippin, they'd named Grey, after Gandalf the Grey. And their daughter had been named after Peregrin, one of Frodo Baggin's best hobbit friends. Pippin for short.

Cassie had never read the books, but she loved her husband.

She wanted no book that had a past to enter their home, but she'd made concessions for Leo. He kept his personal collection under lock and key in the office of the sea captain's house they'd bought in Devil's Cove when they first married. Cassie would have nothing to do with Leo's books, now more than ever. Her fear about what they could tell her about the future was much greater than her temptation.

Her skirt whipped around her legs, billowing out behind her. This weather...the ocean...the Outer Banks of North Carolina. She loved every bit of it. Everything except waiting for Leo to come home to her. Waiting for the sea to give her husband back to her.

They walked together, Pippin's feet moving in double-time to keep up with Cassie's longer stride. "Library!" Pippin yanked on Cassie's hand and pulled her toward the two-story house that had years ago been converted. The word LIBRARY was spelled across the eaves over the small porch entry. A blue sign with a figure holding a book was secured in the ground at the sidewalk, denoting the building as the town's library.

It was a place Cassie never stepped foot into.

"Another day, lovey," she said to Pippin, pulling her along. She placed one hand on her pregnant belly. Through the fog and straight ahead, the town's bookstore came into view. That was another building she refused to go into.

All books had a history.

All books told stories—those written on the pages, and those between the lines.

Cassie wanted nothing to do with any of them.

The library and the bookstore were on opposite sides of the street. If Cassie took the conventional path, she'd have to pass one or the other. Instead, she marked a diagonal to cross the street, leaving the sidewalk before they got to the library, planning to step up onto the opposite sidewalk a few yards past the bookstore. It was the only way to miss them both.

She muttered under her breath. Only her Aunt Rose thought of their family magic as a blessing. To Cassie, it was a curse. Her mother, and her sister Lacy, had both died in childbirth. Her great-grandfather, grandfather, and father had all been taken by the sea. Cassie had left the west coast and the only family she had, only to fall in love with Leonardo Jay Hawthorne, a bookish fisherman from the Outer Banks. Her destiny to live by the sea was fulfilled. She couldn't escape, that was the truth of the matter.

Cassie grabbed hold of Pippin's hand and hurried on, dipping her head against the cold wind. She touched her swollen belly again. She'd survived childbirth, but would she be able to tempt fate twice? And what about Leo. He'd joined the Lane's through marriage, but had Cassie only transferred the curse to him? Would he be able to escape the fate of the men in her family? For that matter, how could she keep Grey off the water and safe?

An elderly woman, her head lowered, emerged from the

bookstore. A cobalt blue scarf covered her hair, its tail whipping behind her. She pulled her woolen coat tight around herself. Instead of staying on the sidewalk, the old woman stepped into the street. Just as Cassie was doing, she cut a diagonal. Cassie looked at the older woman as she and Pippin approached her, gasping when the woman suddenly looked up, her tiger eyes boring into her. A shiver slithered up Cassie's spine.

In an instant, the fog thickened, covering Devil's Cove with a heavy blanket of mist. Something hit the ground as the old woman dropped her gaze again and passed them. Without thinking, Cassie bent to pick up the fallen object. The moment she did, her heart hammered in her chest. She looked at what she held.

It was a tattered copy of Homer's *The Odyssey*.

Cassie cried out. Dropped the book.

It landed on its spine. The pages fell open.

Before Cassie could stop her, Pippin scooped it up and held it out to her, holding it open. "The lady, she dropped it."

Cassie looked over her shoulder. "Wait," she called out, but the fog had swallowed the woman.

A chill swept through Cassie as she looked down at the open pages of the book her daughter held. Her eyes scanned the words and her heart climbed to her throat.

...So all that has been duly done. Listen now, I will tell you
*   all, but the very god himself will make you remember.*
*   You will come first of all to the Sirens, who are enchanters*
*   of all mankind and whoever comes their way; and that man*
*   who unsuspecting approaches them, and listens to the Sirens*
*   singing, has no prospect of coming home and delighting*

    his wife and little children as they stand about him in greeting,

    but the Sirens by the melody of their singing enchant him.

    they sit in their meadow, but the beach before it is piled with the boneheads

    of men now rotted away, and the skins shrivel upon them.

"No. No, no, no." Cassie fell to her knees, unable to hold in her sobs.

Read More...

BOOK MAGIC MYSTERIES

Join my newsletter mailing list and receive a free exclusive copy of *The Bookish Kitchen*, a compilation of recipes from my different series.

Continue with the next Book Magic Mysteries:

ABOUT THE AUTHOR

Melissa Bourbon is the national bestselling author of more than 20 mystery books, including the Lola Cruz Mysteries, A Magical Dressmaking Mystery series, the Bread Shop Mysteries, written as Winnie Archer, and the brand new Book Magic Mysteries.

She is a former middle school English teacher who gave up the classroom in order to live in her imagination full time. Melissa, a California native who has lived in Texas and Colorado, now calls the southeast home. She hikes, practices yoga, cooks, and is slowly but surely discovering all the great restaurants in the Carolinas. Since four of her five amazing kids are living their lives, scattered throughout the country, her dogs, Bean, the pug, and Dobby, the chug, keep her company while she writes.

Melissa lives in North Carolina with her educator husband, Carlos, and their youngest son. She is beyond fortunate to be living the life of her dreams.

VISIT Melissa's website at http://www.melissabourbon.com

JOIN her online book club at https://www.facebook.com/groups/BookWarriors/

JOIN her book review club at https://facebook.com/melissaanddianesreviewclub

ALSO BY MELISSA BOURBON

Book Magic Mysteries

Bread Shop Mysteries, *written as Winnie Archer*

Magical Dressmaking Mysteries

Mystery/Suspense
    Silent Obsession
    Silent Echoes
    Deadly Legends Boxed Set

Paranormal Romance
    Storiebook Charm